A sense of déjà vu washed over me. Less than two weeks earlier I'd discovered Rosalie Schneider, another elderly neighbor, unconscious at the bottom of her basement stairs. I took a few steps into the foyer and turned toward the dimly lit living room. Batty Bentworth sat on her sofa, a multi-colored crocheted granny square afghan draped across her lap, her gaze fixated on the news broadcasting from an old black and white console television set.

"Mrs. Bentworth, didn't you hear me?"

When she didn't respond, I stepped between her and the television. She continued to ignore me, but now I knew why. Batty Bentworth was dead—but not from natural causes.

Acclaim for the Anastasia Pollack Crafting Mysteries
Assault with a Deadly Glue Gun

"Crafty cozies don't get any better than this hilarious confection...Anastasia is as deadpan droll as Tina Fey's Liz Lemon, and readers can't help cheering as she copes with caring for a host of colorful characters." – *Publishers Weekly* (starred review)

"Winston has hit a homerun with this hilarious, laugh-until-your-sides-hurt tale. Oddball characters, uproariously funny situations, and a heroine with a strong sense of irony will delight fans of Janet Evanovich..." – *Booklist* (starred review)

"A comic tour de force." – *ForeWord Magazine* (Book of the Year nominee)

"North Jersey's more mature answer to Stephanie Plum." – *Kirkus Reviews*

"...a delightful romp through the halls of who-done-it." – *The Star-Ledger*

"Make way for Lois Winston's promising new series...I'll be eagerly awaiting the next installment in this thoroughly delightful series." – *Mystery Scene Magazine*

"...once you read the first few pages of Lois Winston's first-in-series whodunit, you're hooked for the duration..." – *Bookpage*

"...madcap but tough-as-nails, no holds barred plot and main character...a step above the usual crafty cozy." – *The Mystery*

Reader

"...Anastasia is, above all, a JERSEY girl..., and never, ever mess with one of them. I can't wait 'til the next book in this series..." – *Suspense Magazine*

"Fans of Stephanie Plum will love Lois Winston's cast of quirky, laughable, and loveable characters." – Brenda Novak, *New York Times* bestselling author.

"What a treat—I can't stop laughing! Witty, wise, and delightfully clever, Anastasia is going to be your new best friend.!" – Hank Phillippi Ryan, Agatha, Anthony, and Macavity award-winning author

"Funny, funny, funny—this is a series you don't want to miss!" – Kasey Michaels, *USA Today* bestselling author

"Anastasia Pollack is as crafty as Martha Stewart, as feisty as Stephanie Plum, and as resourceful as Kinsey Millhone." – Mary Kennedy, author of *The Talk Radio Mysteries*

Death by Killer Mop Doll

"Anastasia is a crafting Stephanie Plum, surrounded by characters sure to bring chuckles..." – *Booklist*

"Several crafts projects, oodles of laughs and an older, more centered version of Stephanie Plum." – *Kirkus Reviews*

"... readers who relish the offbeat will be rewarded." – *Publishers*

"...a 30 Rock vibe...Winston turns out another lighthearted amateur sleuth investigation." – *Library Journal*

"Winston...plays for plenty of laughs...while letting Anastasia shine as a risk-taking investigator who doesn't always know when to quit." — *Alfred Hitchcock Mystery Magazine*

Revenge of the Crafty Corpse

"Fans of craft mysteries will like this, of course, but so will those who enjoy the smart and snarky humor of Janet Evanovich, Laura Levine, and Laura DeSilverio." – *Booklist*

"...a surprisingly fraught stew of jealousy, greed, and sex..." and a "Sopranos-worthy lineup of eccentric characters..." – *Publishers Weekly*

"...amusing characters, a...good mystery and a series of crafting projects featuring cloth yo-yos." – *Kirkus Reviews*

"A fun addition to a series that keeps getting stronger." – *Romantic Times Magazine*

"Chuckles begin on page one and the steady humor sustains a comedic crafts cozy, the third (after *Death by Killer Mop Doll*)... Recommend for Chris Grabenstein ("John Ceepak" series) and Jess Lourey readers." – *Library Journal*

"You'll be both surprised and entertained by this terrific mystery.

I can't wait to see what happens in the Pollack household next." – *Suspense Magazine*

"The book has what a mystery should...It moves along at a good pace...Like all good sleuths, Anastasia pieces together what others don't...The book has a fun twist...and it's clear that Anastasia, the everyday woman who loves crafts and desserts, and has a complete hottie in pursuit, will return to solve another murder and offer more crafts tips..." – *Star-Ledger*

Decoupage Can Be Deadly

"*Decoupage Can Be Deadly* is the fourth in the Anastasia Pollock Crafting Mysteries by Lois Winston. And it's the best one yet. More, please!" – *Suspense Magazine*

"Every single character in these books is awesomely quirky and downright hilarious. This series is a true laugh out loud read!" – Books Are Life–Vita Libri

"This is one of these series that no matter what, I'm going to be laughing my way through a comedy of errors as our reluctant heroine sets a course of action to find a killer while contending with her eccentrically dysfunctional family. This adventure grabs you immediately delivering a fast-paced and action-filled drama that doesn't let up from the first page to the surprising conclusion." – Dru's Book Musings

"Lois Winston's reluctant amateur sleuth Anastasia Pollack is back in another wild romp." – The Book Breeze

Books by Lois Winston

Assault with a Deadly Glue Gun
Death by Killer Mop Doll
Revenge of the Crafty Corpse
Decoupage Can Be Deadly
A Stitch to Die For
Crewel Intentions
Mosaic Mayhem
Patchwork Peril
Crafty Crimes
Definitely Dead
Love, Lies and a Double Shot of Deception
Lost in Manhattan
Someone to Watch Over Me
Talk Gertie to Me
Four Uncles and a Wedding
Hooking Mr. Right
Finding Hope
Elementary, My Dear Gertie
Once Upon a Romance
Finding Mr. Right
Romance Super Bundle
Romance Super Bundle II, Second Chances
Romance Super Bundle III, Always & Forever
Love, Valentine Style
The Magic Paintbrush
House Unauthorized
Bake, Love, Write

A Stitch
to
Die For

LOIS WINSTON

Cover design by L. Winston

ISBN-978-1-940795-30-0

DEDICATION

For Jack, Zoe, Chase, and Collin
who make life so beautiful

ACKNOWLEDGMENTS

Special thanks to Donnell Bell and Irene Peterson for their superb editorial skills.

Thanks also to the various members of Crime Scene Writers, DorothyL, Guppies, and Sisters in Crime who generously volunteer their expertise on an incredible range of topics whenever asked.

And finally, much thanks to plotting weekend hostess Gail Freeman. *A Stitch to Die For* came to life thanks to your incredible generosity and spare bedroom.

ONE

Two weeks ago my mother, Flora Sudberry Periwinkle Ramirez Scoffield Goldberg O'Keefe, took her sixth trip down the aisle to become Flora Sudberry Periwinkle Ramirez Scoffield Goldberg O'Keefe Tuttnauer. The groom's daughter was a no-show. At the time of the ceremony her body was being fished out of the Delaware and Raritan Canal in Lambertville, New Jersey.

Ira Pollack, my stepbrother-in-law and the groom's son-in-law, had just finished a toast to Mama and Lawrence Tuttnauer when two men in dark suits entered the backyard catering tent and headed straight toward him. Given all my dealings with the police over the last few months, I easily made them for detectives, a suspicion confirmed when I spotted them flashing their badges. Ira nodded and followed them out of the tent.

I followed Ira.

He and the two men made their way to the patio at the back of his house. I stopped at the entrance to the tent. The men stood with their backs to me, Ira facing me. From my vantage point I couldn't hear their words over the conversations and music going on behind me, but I saw the color drain from Ira's face. He shook his head violently and yelled, "No!" loud enough for me to hear.

I raced across the lawn as fast as I could in three-inch heels. Once at the patio, I placed my hand on Ira's arm. In a voice that trembled as much as his body, he said, "Cynthia. They found her floating in the canal."

I gasped, then led Ira over to one of the patio lounge chairs. He collapsed onto the cushion and buried his head in his hands as he choked out huge sobs.

I turned to the detectives, waiting for more of an explanation, but both ignored Ira's grief to fixate on the party across the lawn. "What's going on here?" one of them asked.

"A wedding," I said.

"Whose?"

"Ira's father-in-law married my mother."

Both detectives knit their brows together and glared at Ira. "Your wife doesn't show for her father's wedding, and you're not worried?" asked the older and taller of the two men.

Ira tried speaking between sobs. His mouth opened and closed several times, but no words came out. I answered for him. "Cynthia didn't approve of her father marrying my mother."

"And you are?" asked the second detective, whipping out a notepad and pencil.

"Anastasia Pollack. I'm also Ira's stepsister-in-law."

Both detectives repeated the twin eyebrow knit, but neither said anything. Also, up to this point I had no idea how Cynthia had died, so I asked, "What happened to Cynthia?"

"The medical examiner will have to determine cause of death," said the older detective. "We're waiting on an autopsy."

"Do you suspect foul play?"

"Why would you suggest that?" he asked.

I shrugged. "I can't imagine how Cynthia would land in the canal on her own. She isn't...wasn't the canal-strolling type." Dirt and extremely expensive designer duds don't mix.

"What type was she?" asked the younger detective.

Cynthia the Trophy Wife was more the spend-all-day-spending-Ira's-money type. I thought for a moment, not wanting to say anything that might be misconstrued. If Cynthia hadn't died of natural causes, Ira would wind up at the top of the suspect list. "I only met her once," I said, "but I'd describe her as someone more interested in indoor activities than communing with nature."

The spouse is always the prime suspect, but Ira was no killer. The man didn't even have the backbone to discipline his bratty kids. If Cynthia had met with foul play, my money was on the pool boy she'd run off with weeks earlier. "Ira, you have to tell the detectives what happened with Cynthia."

The two men practically pounced on Ira. "Do we need to haul you into headquarters, Mr. Pollack?" asked the older detective.

"It's nothing like that," I said. "Cynthia ran off with her lover."

Ira lifted his tear-streaked face and nodded in confirmation.

"When?" asked the older detective.

"Several weeks ago."

The younger detective headed back to the tent and returned a few minutes later with Mama and Lawrence in tow. Mama had no love for Cynthia, but she was visibly shaken upon learning of her death.

Lawrence, on the other hand, exhibited more anger than grief. "I'm not surprised," he said, shaking his head. "She was always a wild child. Drugs. Cocaine mostly. And alcohol."

Cynthia a cokehead? Maybe that's how she maintained her size zero figure.

The narrow canal path, out of the way and nearly hidden within the wooded area separating the canal from the Delaware River, would make for a perfect spot to deal drugs. I turned to Ira. "Did you know?"

He shook his head. "I had no idea."

"Why didn't you tell him?" I asked Lawrence.

"I had hoped that was all behind her, but..." His voice trailed off. He wrapped an arm around Ira's shoulders. "I'm sorry."

"Do you suspect drugs?" I asked the detectives.

"We'll know more after the autopsy," the older one said. "For now we need Mr. Pollack to make a positive ID of the body."

Ira shuddered, turning green at the thought, but he didn't protest and left willingly. I was surprised the detectives didn't issued a *don't leave town* order to the rest of us before departing, but maybe that only happens on TV and in the movies. Lawrence's bombshell regarding Cynthia's drug habit had put an entirely new spin on their investigation. Ira was probably no longer Suspect Numero Uno.

Even more surprising was Lawrence and Mama's decision to go ahead with their honeymoon. Drugs or not, Lawrence had still just lost his daughter.

"What kind of father takes off on a honeymoon hours after learning of his daughter's death?" I asked Zack on the ride home from the wedding.

Zachary Barnes, professional photojournalist and possible spy, had rented the apartment above my garage last winter shortly after my husband Karl dropped dead in Las Vegas, leaving me with his semi-invalid communist mother and gambling debts equal to the gross national product of Tajikistan.

Zack looks like Pierce Brosnan, George Clooney, Patrick Dempsey, and Antonio Bandares all contributed to his gene pool. I'm a pear-shaped, middle-aged mom of two teenage boys. You'd think we'd have nothing in common. Maybe we don't, but no one told that to our hormones.

This past summer I decided I'd mourned Dead Louse of a Spouse long enough and let nature takes its course with Zack. We'd both been enjoying the trip ever since.

"People handle grief in all sorts of ways," he said.

"I suppose. But it seems rather callous."

Mama hasn't had much luck with husbands since my father drowned while scuba diving in the Yucatan on my parents' twenty-fifth wedding anniversary. Each of her subsequent husbands has met with an unfortunate death not long after their nuptials.

George Ramirez made the unwise and deadly mistake of running with the bulls at Pamplona. Oscar Scoffield succumbed from an allergic reaction to shellfish. Arnie Goldberg lost his footing at the Grand Canyon and plunged to his death. Seamus O'Keefe suffered a fatal cerebral aneurysm when he tried to kiss the Blarney Stone. Lou Beaumont never made it as far as *I do*. Several months ago, shortly after he and Mama announced their engagement, a deranged coworker stabbed him in the heart with one of my knitting needles.

Given her track record, you'd think my mother would be gun-shy about wading into matrimonial waters yet again. Not Mama. Her cockeyed optimism puts Nellie Forbush to shame. She and Lawrence knew each other all of three months before they tied the knot.

~*~

After two weeks in Paris, Mama and Lawrence returned from

their honeymoon, the trip—along with the wedding and their new condo—paid for by Ira. At least this time the groom had survived the honeymoon.

In true Mama fashion they showed up to retrieve Catherine the Great, Mama's corpulent Persian cat, in time to invite themselves to stay for dinner. Mama had also invited Ira and his triple terrors—the interchangeable eleven-year-old twins Melody and Harmony (neither of whom knew a C-sharp from a B-flat) and their nine-year-old brother Isaac. All had arrived before I'd had a chance to kick off my heels after a long day at work.

Luckily, I didn't have to figure out how to stretch a tuna-noodle casserole for four to accommodate an additional six mouths. Ira arrived with enough Chinese take-out to feed half of Westfield. As much as I didn't want a houseful of company on a Monday night, at least I'd have leftovers for the remainder of the week.

"Did you enjoy yourself?" I asked Mama.

"Hardly." She sighed. "I spent the entire trip holding my breath, worrying that something would happen to Lawrence."

"But nothing did," he said, "I told you nothing would."

Mama squeezed his hand. "You can't blame me, given the series of unfortunate events that have plagued my marriages. I swear I'm cursed."

"And now the curse is broken," he said, stooping to plant a peck on her cheek.

I certainly hoped so. Mama deserved some lasting happiness. She and Lawrence made quite the couple, too. My mother bears a striking resemblance to Ellen Burstyn, and Lawrence, with his full head of silver hair, could easily pass for the reincarnation of Cary Grant.

I also harbored ulterior motives for the continued coupling of the newlywed couple. I deserved one less person living under my roof. Mama has moved in with us each time she's lost a husband. My house is a small three-bedroom mid-century rancher, and I'm already stuck with Lucille, the communist mother-in-law from hell. With Mama claiming descent from Russian nobility, the Russian Revolution is still very much alive within the walls of Casa Pollack.

"Have you heard anything further regarding Cynthia's death?" Lawrence asked Ira.

While he and Mama had cavorted along the Seine, the police continued their investigation. Ira had provided me with periodic updates. "You were right about the drugs," he said. "The autopsy results showed massive levels of cocaine and alcohol in her system."

Lawrence shook his head. "I knew it. What about the pool boy? Did he supply her with the drugs?"

"The police don't know."

"Why not?" asked Mama. "Haven't they questioned him?"

According to what the police told Ira, Cynthia and Pablo the Pool Boy had checked into the Lambertville Inn a week before her death. They never checked out. "He's missing," said Ira.

"Of course, he's missing," said Lawrence. "Why would he stick around after killing my daughter? By now he's probably basking on a beach in Venezuela."

"Is that where he comes from?" asked Mama.

Lawrence shrugged. "Who knows?"

"You seem to, dear. Why else would you mention Venezuela?"

"Because it makes perfect sense. He's Latino; he'd head for a Spanish-speaking country. And given the political climate, Venezuela would be a safe haven."

"Why is that?" asked Mama.

"Because they'd most likely ignore an extradition request," said Alex, entering the living room. He kissed his grandmother, waved to Ira and Lawrence, and ignored his cousins who, as usual, were engrossed in their hand-held devices of choice. "Venezuela and the United States haven't been the best of friends the last few years," he explained.

"Someone's been paying attention in civics class," said Lawrence.

"Alex pays attention in all his classes," I said. Before his father had screwed him out of his future, Alex had hoped to attend Harvard next year. Now, thanks to Dead Louse of a Spouse, even community college tuition would be a struggle.

Alex grabbed the bags of food from Ira and followed me into the kitchen. "Why are they all here?" he whispered.

"Your grandmother invited them."

"I have a ton of homework tonight."

"Then you have a perfect excuse to make yourself scarce after dinner."

When Ira first entered our lives a few months ago, my sons had been excited to learn they had cousins. I'm an only child, as was Karl—or so we'd thought. But it turned out Karl's father married and had another son after he and Lucille parted ways. Unfortunately, the excitement of additional family quickly wore off once Alex and Nick met Ira's spoiled brats.

"Where's Nick?" I asked.

"Soccer practice. I finished early." Alex glanced over at the clock on the microwave. "He should be home any minute."

While Alex set the table and I grabbed serving utensils for the food, I wondered what connections, if any, Zack had in Venezuela, assuming he really did work for one of the alphabet agencies. Broaching the subject would get me a swift denial, but that didn't mean he wouldn't look into it on the sly. Spy or not, he seemed to have all sorts of connections in both Washington, DC and around the world.

At the crack of dawn this morning he'd headed to Newark Liberty Airport, supposedly on his way to Amphipolis, Greece to photograph what some scholars argued might be the tomb of Olympias, the mother of Alexander the Great. I had no doubt he'd return with plenty of photographic proof of his destination. What I'd never know was where else he'd gone and what else he'd done.

I try not to ponder the possibilities, but I'm rarely successful. Marriage to the deceitful Dead Louse of a Spouse had ground my Trust gene to pulp, spit it out, and replaced it with a huge dose of skepticism.

Anyway, even though Cynthia had ranked high on the Bitch-O-Meter, no one should get away with murder. So I mulled over a way to bring up the subject with Zack upon his return.

Nick arrived home, and a moment later, like Pavlov's dog, Lucille hobbled into the dining room the instant I placed the first carton of food onto the table. My mother-in-law greeted Ira and his brood with a scowl.

Lucille refuses to believe Ira is her precious Karl's half-brother, even though Ira could almost pass for Karl's twin. Then again, she refuses to believe her precious Karl gambled away his sons' futures and left his family one step away from living in a cardboard box on the street.

She muttered under her breath as she maneuvered herself into a chair at the head of the table, then leaned forward to snag two cardboard containers—a pint of fried rice and a quart of shrimp in lobster sauce, both of which she proceeded to dump onto her plate. Lucille had definitely skipped the section on sharing in *The*

Communist Manifesto.

I hadn't taken my first bite of moo goo gai pan when Ira's cell phone rang. As he reached into his pocket, Melody or Harmony (I'd yet to figure out the difference between the two,) pointed at me and declared in a loud voice, "She said no phones at the table."

I handed down that edict on a previous visit from Ira and his hell spawns after their lack of manners had gotten the better of me. When they at first not only ignored me but gave me lip, I'd grabbed the phones out of their hands and refused to return them until after dinner. I'm glad to see they remembered the rules of the house.

Ira glanced at his phone's display and shrugged. "Sorry, I have to take this call. It's important."

"So are my calls!" His daughter jabbed a finger in my direction. "It's not fair. If I have to follow her stupid rules, everybody has to."

Ignoring her outburst, Ira rose and answered the call as he headed toward the living room.

"If you can, I can," Melody/Harmony shouted after him.

"Me, too," said her sister.

Both girls whipped out their cell phones. Lawrence rose, strode around the table, and plucked the phones from their hands.

"Hey!" said one.

"You can't do that!" said the other.

"I can, and I did," he said, pocketing the phones. "You'll get them back after dinner."

"I hate this stupid house," said Melody, smacking both hands on the table. Or was it Harmony? "And I hate all of you. I don't know why we have to keep coming here."

Lucille glared at her. "The feeling is mutual." Then she targeted me. "This is all your fault, Anastasia. I know you only keep inviting that imposter and his juvenile delinquents to annoy me."

"That's right," said Mama. "The entire world revolves around the commie pinko."

Isaac wadded up his napkin and hurled it at Lucille. It bounced off her head and landed in the middle of her mound of shrimp.

"How dare you!" Lucille picked the soggy napkin from her plate and glared at Isaac. Had he been sitting closer, I have no doubt she would have mashed it into his face. Luckily, he sat beyond her reach. Instead, she growled like her French bulldog Manifesto (AKA Mephisto or Devil Dog) as she dropped the napkin onto the table.

"You have no right to call us names," said Isaac. "We're not juvenile delinquents, you ugly old bitch."

Lucille grabbed her cane and raised it in his direction.

"Go ahead," Ira's son taunted her. "Hit me. I'll call the cops and have you arrested for child abuse. Then I'll sue you for everything you've got."

Mama laughed. "Don't waste your time. She's dead broke, thanks to her son."

Lucille whipped her head around toward Mama. "You leave my son out of this!"

"Open your eyes, you Bolshevik cow. Karl was a lowlife scumbag who screwed you, his wife, and his kids."

"Mama!"

Lucille thought the money she'd kept in shoeboxes under her bed (because she didn't trust banks) had been lost when a fire reduced her apartment building to ashes. According to Ricardo, Karl's loan shark and accomplice, my husband had deliberately set that fire—after he absconded with his mother's life savings. I had never divulged this fact to anyone—especially not to Mama or

Lucille. Had Mama somehow found out, or was she simply taking the opportunity to bait her arch nemesis?

"Well, it's true, isn't it?" she asked in a voice dripping with innocence.

"How dare you sully my son's good name!" said Lucille.

"He sullied his own name long ago," said Mama.

I ignored both my mother and mother-in-law, instead directing my comments to Isaac. "Eat your dinner. You're not old enough to file a lawsuit."

"You're not a lawyer," he said. "And you can't tell me what to do."

"Enough!" Lawrence pounded his fist onto the table. Plates rattled. Water sloshed around in glasses. "You kids can either behave yourselves or go sit in your father's car until he's ready to leave."

He then turned to Mama, "Flora, dear, I suggest you and Anastasia's mother-in-law bury the hatchet once and for all for everyone's sake."

Mama glared at Lucille. "She started it."

I didn't need to be a mind reader to see the thought bubble hovering above Mama's strawberry blonde waves. She'd be happy to bury the hatchet—right in Lucille's skull.

"Actually, dear," said Lawrence, "you started it."

Mama gasped. "You're supposed to take my side, not that leftist pinko's!"

Lawrence patted her hand. "Only when you're right, Flora. Now I suggest we all calm down and finish our dinner."

Mama looked as though Lawrence had slapped her across the face. Lucille smirked before turning her attention back to her mound of shrimp. I guess Ira's kids enjoyed the Chinese food too much to give up dinner because the three of them remained at the table. By the time Ira returned to the dining room they all sat silently hunched over their plates while they gobbled down egg rolls and shoveled huge forkfuls of lo mein into their mouths.

"The police found Pablo," said Ira.

"In Venezuela?" asked Mama.

"In a Dumpster in Camden. He was strangled with a bicycle lock."

TWO

"Cool!" said Isaac. "Just like in *Breaking Bad*. Are there pictures?"

"Euw!" said one of his sisters.

"Gross!" said the other.

I stared at Ira, horrified that he'd permit a nine-year-old access to such a violent television series. Even though my kids are teenagers, I had refused to allow them to watch *Breaking Bad* during the original series run and still wouldn't permit them to view it now that it was in reruns and on demand.

Noticing my appalled expression, Lawrence said, "It was a great show—superb writing, acting, and directing—even if it was a bit violent."

"A *bit* violent?" Not from what I'd heard.

"Well, I suppose more than a bit." Then he added, "but totally inappropriate for children."

Color rose up Ira's neck and into his cheeks. He averted his gaze, suddenly taking extreme interest in the mound of white rice heaped on his plate.

I glanced at my sons, curious to see their reactions. They both shook their heads and rolled their eyes. They'd come to realize Ira had little common sense when it came to his kids.

"He did it," said Lucille, stabbing her fork in Ira's direction. "Had them both killed. You'll see. I told you not to trust him." She then slid her empty plate toward the middle of the table and hoisted herself up from her chair.

"You watch out, Anastasia," she said as she hobbled from the dining room. "That man just might murder you in your sleep, and it will serve you right for bringing him into this house."

The flush of scarlet that had colored Ira's face and neck quickly drained away, leaving in its place a ghostly pallor. His entire body shook. He dropped his fork on his plate and mumbled at his rice, "I...I had noth...nothing to do w...with Cynthia's death." Then, almost as an afterthought, added, "Or Pablo's."

Ira was either delivering an Oscar-worthy performance, or he was telling the truth. From everything I'd come to know about him, I held fast to my opinion that he was no cold-blooded killer.

"So Pablo was executed," said Lawrence.

Apparently, Ira wasn't the only person at the dinner table who lacked discretion. Ira's kids had finished their dinner. I turned to my sons. "Why don't you take Isaac and the twins into the den?"

"What about dessert?" asked Isaac.

"There are apples in a bowl on the kitchen table," I said. "Help yourselves."

"Fruit? That's not dessert," said one of the girls. "What about ice cream?"

"Or brownies?" asked Isaac.

"Unless you brought some with you, you're out of luck," I said.

"This house sucks," said Isaac. "It's like a prison. I want to leave. Now!"

"You'll go home when you're father's ready to leave," said Lawrence. He handed the girls back their phones. "Go into the den, or go sit in the car."

"Dad," whined one of the girls, "tell him to stop ordering us around."

Ira glanced at his daughter, then at Lawrence. "Do as your grandfather says."

"He's not our grandfather!" said Isaac, stamping his foot. "He can't tell us what to do."

"I'm telling the three of you to listen to him," said Ira. "Go into the den. Finish your homework, and we'll stop for ice cream on the way home."

Having gotten the promise of dessert, Ira's three kids grabbed the backpacks they'd dumped on my foyer floor and headed for the den.

"Do we have to babysit them?" asked Nick. "I've got homework."

"Me, too," said Alex.

And I had both a massive case of indigestion and a pounding headache. No matter how often I'd told Mama she couldn't invite Ira and his brood to my home without first consulting me, she continued to do so. By her way of thinking, her need to annoy Lucille trumped my need for less conflict in my life.

I'd have to make it clear to Ira that no matter what Mama said, he needed to clear all invitations with me first—especially during the week. I shook my head. "No need. Go do your homework."

Once all the kids had dispersed, Lawrence pumped Ira for more information concerning the call he'd received, "What else did the cops say?"

Ira absent-mindedly pushed some rice noodles around on his

plate but made no effort to load his fork with any food. "They think it was gang-related. Probably a territorial dispute."

Camden claimed the dubious distinction of ranking the highest of any city in the country—higher even than Newark or Detroit—for violent crime. Anyone with an ounce of common sense stays far away from what's been dubbed the most dangerous city in America.

"Where does that leave their investigation into Cynthia's death?" asked Lawrence.

"They didn't say."

They never do. Over the last few months, thanks to my involvement in several other murder investigations, I'd often heard the standard cop non-answer of "I can't comment on an ongoing investigation."

At least now I no longer needed to ask Zack about his Venezuelan connections. However, unless the police could tie Pablo's murder to Cynthia's death, their only lead was now a dead end—literally. "Cynthia's and Pablo's deaths may not be connected," I said.

"How can they not be?" asked Ira.

"Anastasia is right," said Lawrence. "Cynthia wasn't murdered. She died of an overdose. She probably fell into the canal, or Pablo panicked and dumped her body there after she died."

"Unless someone wanted her death to look like an overdose," I said.

"Like Pablo?" asked Mama.

Lawrence shook his head. "He had nothing to gain by murdering my daughter. No one did. I'm sure the police will eventually rule her death an accidental overdose. Pablo may have supplied her with drugs, but Cynthia was a victim of her own vices."

"We don't know that Pablo was Cynthia's dealer," I said. "He may not have had anything to do with her death."

"You're forgetting they checked into the inn together, and drugs were found in their room," said Lawrence.

"What if they got into a fight?" I asked. "Pablo may have walked out on her before she overdosed."

Lawrence laughed. "Be serious. She was his meal ticket. Why would he walk out on her?"

The answer seemed obvious to me if not to Lawrence. "She wasn't much of a meal ticket once Ira cut off her credit cards. Why would he stay?"

"Anastasia's right," said Mama. "Listen to her. She knows all about solving murders. She's had lots of experience."

"She's hardly a law enforcement professional," said Lawrence, "just someone who's repeatedly stuck her nose in places that got her in trouble."

Hmm...I was beginning to sense Lawrence had as little love for me as I had for him.

Mama ignored his comment and turned to me. "Maybe you should offer your services to the police, dear."

"I'm sure they're handling things well enough without me, Mama. Anyway," I continued, staring pointedly at Lawrence, "there are many possible scenarios. Right now all anyone has are assumptions based on circumstantial evidence. No proof of anything. I doubt the police are ready to close their investigation."

"Well, I disagree," said Lawrence. "I think it's obvious what happened. My daughter overdosed on drugs supplied by Pablo. He panicked, dumped her body in the canal, and fled. As for what happened to him, he was probably trying to horn in on someone else's territory."

"What makes you so sure Pablo was a drug dealer?" I asked. "We have no proof of that."

Lawrence sneered at me. "How could he not be? Cynthia had to get her drugs from someone."

"Perhaps she had her own connections," I said. "You told us she'd done drugs for years." I turned to Ira. "How long has Pablo worked for you?"

Ira shrugged. "I have no idea. He worked for the pool service I contract with, but I don't remember seeing him before this summer."

"Which means he probably wasn't her supplier," I said. "Not if she'd been using drugs before and throughout her marriage to Ira."

"Has the medical examiner released Cynthia's body yet?" asked Mama, changing the subject slightly. "We'll need to plan her funeral."

"Last Wednesday," said Ira. "I had her cremated the following day."

"Then we'll go with a memorial service," said Mama, the Martha Stewart of funeral planning, thanks to her vast experience with spouses dying on her.

"We decided that under the circumstances a service would be inappropriate," said Lawrence.

"When did you decide that?" asked Mama.

"Before you and I left for Paris."

"What about Cynthia's sister?" I asked. "Didn't she want to pay her respects?"

"What sister?" asked Lawrence. "Cynthia was an only child."

I suppose that explained why Cynthia's sister was a no-show at Lawrence and Mama's wedding. I'd assumed she'd stayed away from the nuptials in solidarity with Cynthia.

"Ira," I said, "the day we met you told us Cynthia was out of town visiting her sister."

"You must have misunderstood," he mumbled into his plate.

"I don't think so." I turned to Mama. "You remember, don't you, Mama?"

"I'm afraid I don't, dear."

Well, I did. I clearly remembered the conversation, plus the one a few days later when Ira said he had to leave to pick Cynthia up at the airport. Why had he lied? "So who was Cynthia visiting back then?" I asked.

Ira refused to make eye contact with me. "I may have said she'd gone to visit a *sorority* sister."

He hadn't. At the time I didn't know Cynthia was Ira's trophy wife and his kids' stepmother. Had he mentioned a sorority sister, I would have thought it odd for a mother to choose visiting a friend over attending Parents' Day at her children's overnight camp. "Was she?"

He pulled at his tie and loosened his collar before mumbling, "Not exactly."

I let the subject drop. Ira's refusal to look at me, along with his fidgeting body language, suggested Cynthia had been off cavorting with her pool boy lover.

~*~

By the time everyone not living under the Casa Pollack roof had departed for their own homes, a heavy metal percussion band had taken up residence between my temples. I put away the leftover Chinese food, turned my back on the dirty dishes still piled on the dining room table, and headed for the boys' bedroom.

"I need you guys to load the dishwasher for me."

Nick glanced up from his chemistry book. "You look kind of green, Mom."

"That's why I need your help. I've got a date with two Motrin and a steamy bath."

"How do we keep Uncle Ira and his kids from dropping in all the time?" asked Alex.

"Short of gagging your grandmother? I'm not sure."

"Now that grandma's married to Lawrence, we're going to see a lot more of Ira and his kids, aren't we?"

I sighed. "I'm afraid so."

~*~

"How are the newlyweds?" asked Cloris the next morning at work. "Did the groom survive?"

Cloris McWerther is the food editor at *American Woman*, the magazine where I work as the crafts editor. Our cubicles are across the hall from each other. However, Cloris is much more than merely a coworker. She's the Dr. Watson to my amateur Sherlocking, even saving my life once when another coworker tried to kill me.

She also keeps me from starving, given that I often don't have time for breakfast in the morning and usually work through lunch. Unfortunately, the sustenance she provides is generally of the baked goods variety—disastrous to both my lack of willpower and my spreading hips. Today's offering consisted of an assortment of liqueur-infused donuts supplied by a new bakery in Union Square. I immediately zeroed in on the chocolate-glazed Chambord confection. The combination of chocolate and raspberries will be my downfall. Spike the two with alcohol, and I'm doomed to suffer from Spreading Hip Syndrome for the rest of my life.

Cloris receives a constant stream of edible swag from vendors hoping for editorial showcasing in our magazine. Me? My swag consists of calorie-free but definitely inedible felt squares, chenille stems, and pompoms. Life can be so unfair.

As I savored the donut, I caught Cloris up on the events of last evening. "I'm glad Mama has found someone who makes her happy; I just wish he didn't come with so much dysfunctional family baggage. I have enough of that from Lucille."

"If you're referring to Ira and his family, you'd have them with or without Lawrence in the picture."

Something else I can blame on my not-so-dearly-departed husband. Thanks to Karl, I'm not only stuck with his curmudgeonly mother and debt up the wazoo, I now have his needy half-brother and those bratty kids in my life. How lucky can one girl get? "At least they live nearly an hour away."

"Did you ever stop to consider that Ira might not be who he appears?" asked Cloris.

"What do you mean?"

"Karl fooled everyone. Ira is Karl's brother—"

"Half-brother."

Cloris waved away the distinction. "Whatever. Maybe Karl and Ira share more than just looks. What if Ira's insecurities and neediness are all a carefully crafted cover for a more sinister personality?"

The idea struck me as absurd. "You think Ira staged Cynthia's murder to look like an accidental overdose? And then executed Pablo?"

Cloris shrugged. "Stranger things have happened. Need I remind you that John List lived in your town? Who would ever have expected such a milquetoast of a man to murder his wife, mother, and two kids?"

"That happened nearly forty years ago."

"So? Watch the news. Similar crimes happen every day all across America, and the perpetrators often look more like Clark

Kent than Charles Manson."

Once upon a time I would have accused Cloris of watching too many crime dramas on TV, but that was before my life spiraled into a crime drama. As much as I hated to admit it, she did have a point. After all, how much did I really know about Ira other than what he himself had told me? "I suppose anything is possible. Pablo may have been dumped in Camden, not killed there."

"The medical examiner would be able to determine that."

"I'm sure he has, but according to Ira, the police aren't releasing any specific information. All we know is that Pablo was found in Camden."

"All *you* know. Ira may know quite a bit more."

Great. Now I had to worry whether or not I'd allowed a cold-blooded killer into my home.

I licked Chambord-spiked raspberry jam from my fingers and reached for another donut, one labeled Peach Margarita. Maybe the sugar rush would switch out the visions of a possibly murderous stepbrother-in-law swimming around in my brain with images of rainbows and unicorns. A girl can hope, right? Otherwise I'd spend my day going crazy with conjecture and worry when I needed to concentrate on preparing for our upcoming editorial meeting.

The *American Woman* editors meet the last Monday of each month to present status reports on all the issues in various stages of production. In addition, we pick the theme for the issue next up in the queue. Even though part of the meeting involves brainstorming new ideas, I always like to prepare a few ahead of time. In the past, some of the chosen themes hadn't easily lent themselves to craft projects, causing me considerable stress. I already have enough stress in my life.

According to the cupcake-themed calendar hanging above

Cloris's computer, I had less than a week to come up with an idea Naomi would love enough to choose. I wondered how she felt about rainbows and unicorns. "Have you given any thought to the next issue?" I asked.

"Not really. I can create a cake for whatever theme Naomi decides on."

"You're no help."

"Talk to Jeanie."

Jeanie Sims was our decorating editor. An earth mother who dressed in denim and Birkenstocks, she loved themes where she could incorporate recycling and upcycling. We worked well together.

"Talk to Jeanie about what?"

"Speak of the devil," said Cloris as Jeanie joined us in Cloris's cubicle and snagged a Limoncello donut.

"A theme for the next issue," I said. "Any ideas?"

"As a matter of fact, I do. We haven't featured an issue on babies in over a year. I'd love to create a shabby chic nursery from salvaged items."

"What about lead paint?" asked Cloris.

"I'd stress first using a lead paint test kit on all the items."

"Janice could write an article about the dangers of lead paint in older homes." I said, referring to Janice Kerr, our health editor. "That would tie in nicely."

"I could create a menu for a baby shower," said Cloris.

They both turned to me. One of my biggest challenges was coming up with projects that didn't require multiple pages of patterns. Readers wanted full-size patterns; the bean counters hated full-size patterns. They didn't like giving me any more editorial space than necessary because I didn't pull in huge advertising dollars the way fashion and beauty did. According to the bean counters, a successful issue was one where the sales department sold so much advertising that I lost editorial pages.

"I haven't featured a knitting or crochet project in quite some time," I said. "I can design an infant layette."

"Naomi will love it," said Cloris.

"Tessa will hate it," said Jeanie, referring to our prima donna fashion editor.

Cloris smirked. "All the more reason to do it. We'll get Janice on board and go into next Monday's meeting as a united front."

~*~

After nearly an hour of battling rush hour traffic, I finally arrived home, relieved to find neither Ira's van nor Lawrence's car parked at the curb. After last night's chaos, I looked forward to a relatively peaceful dinner—*relatively* being the operative word. After all, I never knew what to expect from my mother-in-law.

However, as I turned to head into the house, an unexpected shaft of bright light caught my eye. Across the street, Betty Bentworth's door stood half ajar, the glow from her foyer chandelier spilling out onto her front porch.

Betty—otherwise known as Batty Bentworth—spent her life seated in front of her living room window where she spied on her neighbors. She kept the Westfield police on speed dial, often calling multiple times a day to complain about anything and everything, once even demanding the arrest of her six-year-old next-door neighbor for vandalism. The child's crime? She'd drawn a chalk hopscotch board on the sidewalk in front of Betty's house.

Batty Bentworth was not someone who left her front door open—especially after dark.

Like everyone else in the neighborhood, I kept my distance from Mrs. Bentworth. You never knew what would set her off, and it was best not to get on her bad side. Not that she had a good side from what I knew of her.

Still, I couldn't ignore that open door. Rather than head across the street, I decided to call her. Maybe she'd gone out earlier to retrieve her mail, and the door hadn't latched completely when she returned. The stiff October breeze blowing down the street may have pushed the door open.

I whipped out my cell phone, scrolled to her number, and placed the call. The phone rang. And rang. And rang. After a dozen rings I hung up, sighed, and reluctantly crossed the street.

"Hello? Mrs. Bentworth?" I called through the open door. No answer. I shouted her name. "Mrs. Bentworth!" Only the sound of the six o'clock news blaring from her television greeted me.

I stepped inside and shouted above the Eyewitness News reporter. "Mrs. Bentworth! It's Anastasia Pollack. Your front door is open."

A sense of déjà vu washed over me. Less than two weeks earlier I'd discovered Rosalie Schneider, another elderly neighbor, unconscious at the bottom of her basement stairs. I took a few steps into the foyer and turned toward the dimly lit living room. Batty Bentworth sat on her sofa, a multi-colored crocheted granny square afghan draped across her lap, her gaze fixated on the news broadcasting from an old black and white console television set.

"Mrs. Bentworth, didn't you hear me?"

When she didn't respond, I stepped between her and the television. She continued to ignore me, but now I knew why. Batty Bentworth was dead—but not from natural causes.

THREE

Betty Bentworth had taken a bullet to her eye. A dark trickle of dried blood ran down her cheek and pooled on top of the arthritic right hand that rested in her lap. Her left hand still held the handle of a coffee cup, the cup's contents now forming a circular stain on the sofa cushion. I'm no crime scene investigator, but even I could deduce from her calm pose that Betty never heard or saw the killer approach.

I glanced around the room. Although I'd never before entered Betty's home, nothing appeared out of place. There was no evidence of ransacking or burglary. Ornate silver candlesticks graced the fireplace mantle. Her coffee table held a matching five-piece silver tea service. The silver seemed incongruous with the sparse, decades-old threadbare furniture of the room. Unless the killer came for something specific and knew exactly where to find it, this certainly didn't have the markings of a burglary gone wrong. To my untrained eye and because I live in New Jersey, this looked like a hit to me.

But why? Betty Bentworth was a royal pain in the patoutie to everyone on the block, not to mention the Westfield police, but no more so than my own mother-in-law. What had the disagreeable octogenarian done to warrant a bullet to the head? Who could possibly hate her that much?

Since such close proximity to a murder victim sent shivers of dread up and down my spine, I rushed back outside before calling the police.

"911. State your emergency."

"My neighbor's been shot. She's dead." I gave my name and Betty's address.

"Are you certain she's dead, ma'am?"

"Positive."

"Are you in any danger?"

"I don't think so. It looks like she was killed several hours ago."

"How do you know that, ma'am?"

"The blood on her face is dry."

"I see. Are you still on the premises?"

"I'm standing on the sidewalk in front of her house."

"Stay there. A squad car is on the way."

Over the years Westfield, like many suburban towns, experienced the occasional homicide. However, with few exceptions, most recently being the murders that occurred a few months ago at the Westfield Assisted Living and Rehabilitation Center, the majority of these murders were crimes of passion committed by husbands or boyfriends. A gruesome murder occurring less than a week before Halloween belonged in a horror movie, not in Westfield, New Jersey.

I had no love for Halloween. Real life was scary enough. The makeshift sheet-ghosts tied to my neighbors' tree limbs and whipping around in the wind added to my unease, as did the skeletons and gravestones dotting many of the front yards and the creepy-faced jack-o-lanterns shining from porches and windows. I knew it was all fake, but as I stood on the sidewalk, dried leaves swirling around my feet, I also knew a killer had been here recently. Images of Michael Myers and Freddy Krueger flashed before me.

Thankfully, less than two minutes after placing my call to 911, a Westfield squad car, lights flashing but sirens silent, pulled up to the curb. I shook off my Halloween phobia as officers Harley and Fogarty stepped from the vehicle. The two cops and I had come to know each other quite well over the last year, thanks to the upheaval in my life. When they stepped from the squad car, their expressions telegraphed their lack of surprise at finding I was the neighbor who had called in the report.

Both officers towered over me, but that's where their physical similarities ended. Fogarty sported a body-builder's physique. Although currently hidden by a leather jacket, on previous occasions I'd seen his muscles strain the seams of his uniform. Harley's body also strained his seams but more from pudginess than muscle.

"Someone shot Batty Bentworth?" asked Harley, the older of the two by about ten years.

I nodded.

"Mrs. Pollack, you really need to stop stumbling across dead bodies," said Fogarty.

"I'd like nothing better. I never set out to become the Jessica Fletcher of Westfield."

"Could've fooled me," said Harley. "You're racking up some decent crime-solving stats. We may have to deputize you."

"No, thanks."

Fogarty scoped out the front of Betty's house. "So the old bat's really dead?"

I nodded. "Bullet to her head."

"Wait here while we check things out," said Harley.

The two officers headed inside the house. A moment later an unmarked car and a Crime Scene Investigation van, both with flashing lights, pulled up behind the squad car.

While the officers from the van grabbed their gear and hurried down the walkway to Betty's front door, a rotund man pried himself from behind the wheel of the unmarked car and stepped into the street. He took one look at me and said, "You again?"

"Nice to see you, too, Detective."

Detective Samuel Spader—no joke—and I had met over the summer when my mother-in-law was the prime suspect in the strangulation death of her roommate at the Westfield Assisted Living and Rehabilitation Center. Spader was not the first ironic name I'd come across in law enforcement. Over the past few months I'd interacted with Detectives Batswin and Robbins in Morris County and Detectives Phillips and Marlowe in Manhattan. I chalked up the coincidence of their names and chosen careers to the universe needing to provide me with an occasional laugh, given all the crap it had dumped on me recently.

Sam Spader was a heart attack waiting to happen. When doctors told him the stress of working homicide in Newark would kill him sooner than a bullet, he'd transferred to Union County to finish out his years before retirement. However, judging from what I'd observed of him, he had more to fear from liquor, cigarettes, and donuts than bullets. His nose sported the burst capillaries of a man who drank too much, nicotine stained his fingers and teeth, and he wore an enormous spare tire around his middle. If he didn't clean up his act, he'd never make it to retirement, no matter in which jurisdiction he worked.

"You find the vic?" he asked.

"I did."

"I'm going to need a statement from you. Wait here." He then lumbered toward the entrance to the house.

The flashing lights eventually drew the attention of various neighbors. One by one they exited their decorated homes and converged on me. With the wind picking up and the mercury plummeting, they created a much-appreciated windbreak around me.

"What's going on?" asked Angie Perotta, the mother of the hopscotch aficionado.

Even though I was totally freaked at the thought of a murderer in the neighborhood, I knew the police wouldn't appreciate me divulging the details of Betty's death. "Mrs. Bentworth died," I said.

"Good riddance."

Others nodded or murmured in agreement. Perhaps they'd feel more sympathetic—not to mention scared as hell—once they learned the cause of Betty's death. For now, they'd have to wait to read the salacious details in tomorrow's newspaper unless Spader saw fit to tell them. Once they knew, we'd all take part in a town-wide freak-out.

Until then, since no one had any love for the deceased, and most had left their homes without first grabbing jackets, the crowd quickly dispersed. I was left alone to shiver in the cold as I waited to give my statement.

A minute later Lawrence's gold Honda Accord pulled up in front of my house. Mama jumped out of the car and raced across the street before Lawrence cut the engine. "Anastasia, thank God you're safe! I was so worried."

"I'm fine, Mama. Why are you here?"

"What do you mean, why am I here? You've got a killer loose on your street. I was worried."

"How in the world did you find out?" Even the press hadn't arrived yet, but somehow my mother had gotten wind of Betty Bentworth's murder.

"Lawrence heard the call go out on his police scanner."

By this time Lawrence had joined us. Dressed for the arctic, he wore a bulky pea coat, a muffler wrapped around the lower part of his face, and a fur-lined leather bombardier hat covering his head. With the brim pulled down over his forehead, only his eyes showed. At least one of us was protected against frostbite. "You listen to a police scanner?" I asked.

"It's a hobby of mine," he said, his voice muffled by the muffler.

Stamp collecting is a hobby. Cooking is a hobby. Beekeeping is a hobby. Monitoring police radio bandwidths struck me as more voyeurism than a hobby. I still knew little more than zilch about my new stepfather but could think of only one reason he might listen in on police dispatches. "Were you in law enforcement before you retired?" I asked.

Mama latched onto her husband's arm, craned her neck toward him, and beamed. "Lawrence owned a very successful commercial laundry service."

Very successful? The only difference between Lawrence and Mama's other husbands—besides the fact that he was still breathing—was that he had his very own sugar daddy in the guise of Ira "Moneybags" Pollack. What had happened to the fruits of Lawrence's successful enterprise? Maybe Ira knew.

Anyway, I saw no connection between soapsuds and the

police. Perhaps Lawrence had wanted to be a cop when he was a kid and now derived some vicarious thrill out of eavesdropping on police communications.

At that moment Detective Spader emerged from Betty's house and headed down the flagstone walkway toward me. "Mama, I need to give the detective my statement. Why don't you and Lawrence wait in the house for me."

"But—"

I cast pleading eyes toward Lawrence. My fingers and toes had turned numb from the cold, and my teeth were beginning to chatter. I'd get through my statement in far less time without Mama standing next to me, interrupting every other sentence to offer her two cents worth of nonsense.

"Come, Flora." He grasped her upper arm and practically dragged her back across the street.

"Really, Lawrence," she protested, "someone should stay with Anastasia."

"She's a big girl. She can take care of herself."

Spader lit a cigarette and took several deep drags as he watched Lawrence and Mama head toward my house. I sidestepped his smoke, although part of me wanted to cup my hands around the glowing cigarette tip to steal some of its warmth.

When Mama and Lawrence were out of earshot, Spader shoved the cigarette to the side of his mouth and whipped out a small spiral notebook and pencil stub. "Harley and Fogarty tell me the vic had lots of enemies. I take it you weren't one of them?"

"I wouldn't say we were enemies. I've had a few minor skirmishes with her from time to time—as have all the neighbors on the block—but nothing the last several years. Like everyone else, I tried to keep my distance."

"But you found her. Did you have a key?"

I quickly explained what had happened. "No one liked her, but I don't know that she had enemies, at least not the kind that go around shooting people in the head."

"Why was she so disliked?"

I shrugged. "Betty Bentworth was a disagreeable, nasty old woman who did nothing but complain, criticize, and threatened lawsuits."

"Over what?"

"You name it—a dog peeing on her lawn, someone parking in front of her house—"

"Anyone can park on the street," he said.

"Not according to Betty. She insisted the street in front of her house belonged to her. Anyone who parked in that spot received a threatening note stuck under the car's windshield wiper. Same with the sidewalk." I told him about the hopscotch incident.

"Was there anyone who liked her?"

"No one I know. Any attempts at friendship were met with suspicion and quickly rebuffed. She was nasty to everyone and had been that way for as long as I've lived here."

I pondered for a moment, then added, "Maybe something happened to her years ago, or maybe she was born with a mean streak. Who knows? You have to feel sorry for people like that."

"Someone didn't." Spader took another drag, hacking once before he continued. "You have any idea who might have wanted her dead?"

I laughed in spite of the situation. "Probably everyone on the police force. She kept 911 on speed dial."

Spader stepped closer. Looming over me, he set his mouth in a tight line and narrowed his eyes. "Are you suggesting—?"

I took a step backward. "No, of course not." The man must

have been on a smoke break when God handed out the Sense of Humor genes.

"Hmm. What about the neighbors? Anyone who might have had a beef big enough to turn to murder?"

"Unlikely. This is a block of mostly teachers, lawyers, and accountants."

"You sure of that?"

I thought about the twelve houses on our one-block-long street and the people who lived in them. No one stood out as the hit man type, but I'd had enough run-ins with hit men lately to know they came in all sizes and shapes. Still, I didn't see any of my neighbors as possible assassins. "Pretty sure."

"How well do you know your neighbors, Mrs. Pollack?"

"I suppose about as well as most people know their neighbors. We wave hello to each other, chitchat while raking leaves, often attend the same school functions. That sort of thing."

"In other words, you really don't know any of them very well at all, do you?"

In the dim light of the street lamp I studied Spader's face. He looked dead serious. Earlier in the day Cloris had planted doubts about Ira in my head. Now Spader was suggesting I might have a homicidal maniac or hired gun living on my street. "Is there something I should know about one of my neighbors, Detective?"

"Not that I'm aware of."

"Then why scare the crap out of me?" Not to mention turn me as suspicious as Betty Bentworth. Had her paranoia been justified? Did she know something about one of our neighbors that I didn't? Something that had gotten her killed?

Spader ignored my question. He took one last drag from his cigarette, tossed the butt onto the sidewalk, and ground it to death with the toe of his shoe. "If Mrs. Bentworth were still alive and had seen you do that, she'd threaten to sue you for sullying her sidewalk."

"Sounds like she was a real piece of work."

"If you want confirmation, ask anyone on the police force."

"So, Nancy Drew, what's your theory?"

The detective had developed a grudging respect for me when I discovered a clue he and his team had missed while investigating the death of Lyndella Wegner this past summer. The Nancy Drew snark aside, I think he genuinely wanted to know my thoughts on Betty's murder.

"I don't think she ever knew what hit her. She certainly didn't let her assailant into the house."

"How do you know that?"

"I discovered the body, remember? And you've seen it. She was watching TV. Betty was hard of hearing and had the television volume turned up high. I'm guessing she didn't hear him break in through a window or the back door."

"There was no evidence of forced entry. She must have let him in."

I glanced longingly over at my own front door, anxious for the warmth behind it, and shoved my numb bare fingers under my armpits. "And left her front door wide open? Not Betty. Maybe the killer left the front door open when he ran out." But that seemed odd to me. Why would he risk someone seeing him leave? Sneaking out the back door made more sense.

"If she didn't let him in, and she kept her doors locked—"

"Paranoid people definitely keep their doors locked, and Betty wasn't someone who would open her door to a stranger."

"She may have forgotten to lock the door."

"Doubtful. She wasn't the forgetful type. The woman held onto grudges for decades."

"Did she show any signs of dementia?"

"None. If the killer didn't force his way in, he must have picked a lock and sneaked up on her."

"But why?"

"I don't know. Maybe she inadvertently witnessed something."

"And someone wanted to make sure she didn't talk? Not a bad theory, Mrs. Pollack. But where was she, and what did she see?"

"That's your job to figure out, isn't it, Detective?"

Spader flipped his notebook closed and shoved it in his breast pocket. Then he reached into his pants pocket, pulled out a card, and handed it to me. "If you think of anything else, call me."

As I accepted the card, he added, "One other thing. Do you have any security cameras on your property?"

"One at each door." After several break-ins last winter, Zack had insisted on installing an alarm system and cameras under the guise of protecting the expensive photographic equipment he kept in his apartment above my detached garage. He claimed the added cost to include the house was negligible. Although I didn't believe him, I hardly put up an argument. As much as I never again wanted to rely on a man, finding my family trussed up with duct-taped and tossed into the bathtub was incentive enough to accept all the help I could get to ward off attacks from any future bad guys.

"Mind if I look at the tape in a little while?" asked Spader.

"Not at all. Stop by when you're ready."

By this time I had lost the battle to keep my eyes from tearing, my nose from running, and my teeth from chattering. As Spader headed back into Betty's house, I raced across the street. Through my closed front door, I heard Lucille and Mama squaring off in the living room.

FOUR

"You're nothing but a vapid, worthless excuse for a human being!"

"You should talk, you traitorous pinko pig!"

So intent on hurling venomous insults at each other, neither Mama nor Lucille noticed me when I stepped into the foyer. Ralph, my Shakespeare-quoting African Grey parrot, sat atop the bookcase, his head swiveling back and forth as he followed the verbal fisticuffs. "*Braaawwk!*" he squawked. "*Mortal revenge upon these traitorous Goths. And see their blood, or die with this reproach. Titus Andronicus.* Act Four, Scene One."

"Déjà vu all over again," I muttered under my breath, choosing a more modern-day quote from New Jersey's favorite son Yogi Berra. I walked past Mama and Lucille and headed into the kitchen where I grabbed the leftover Chinese food from the refrigerator, emptied the containers into casserole dishes, and popped them into the oven.

My sons waylaid me as I passed the den on my way to my bedroom. "Mom," said Alex. "Lawrence said someone shot Batty

Bentworth."

"Right here on our street," added Nick.

I stepped into the den. Lawrence sat on the couch watching the news, apparently totally oblivious to his wife and my mother-in-law setting off World War III in my living room. Or maybe he was deliberately tuning out the battle.

"As scary as it is to know someone on our street was murdered," I reassured my sons, "I don't think we need to worry. It appears Mrs. Bentworth was deliberately targeted."

"I guess she pissed off the wrong person this time," said Nick. He turned to his brother. "Maybe Mom's right."

"About what?" I asked.

"You're always saying if you don't have something nice to say, don't say anything. That woman was despicable."

"And now she's dead," said Alex.

"That's a pretty drastic example." Inwardly, though, I patted myself on the back, glad my sons listened to me and appreciated my parenting skills.

"Maybe someone should tell Grandmother Lucille there's a serial killer on the loose, and he's stalking disagreeable old crones," suggested Nick.

"You think it would help?" asked Alex.

Nick shrugged. "Couldn't hurt."

I glanced down the hall. "One of these days those two might just harangue each other to death."

"If they don't come to physical blows first," said Lawrence, pulling himself away from a newscast about an earthquake in Argentina. Maybe he wasn't so oblivious after all.

"Would you try talking some sense into Mama?" I asked. "She won't listen to me."

"I think she derives a certain amount of pleasure in baiting

Lucille," he said, stating what the rest of us in the family had known for years.

"Perverse pleasure. But it only makes my life more difficult. She no longer has to live with Lucille; I do."

"I'll talk to her," he said, "but I doubt she'll stop until Lucille is dead and buried."

"That's what I'm afraid of." Then, even though I already knew the answer, I asked, "Are you and Mama planning to stay for dinner?"

"Since we're already here, we'll help you polish off all those leftovers from last night."

Leftovers I had hoped would stretch for more than one dinner this week. Even without a murder on the street, Mama and Lawrence had probably planned to show up in time for dinner tonight. No matter how often I tried to impress my near-destitute situation on Mama, she seemed incapable of comprehending the financial realities of my post-Karl life.

As for Lawrence, the man had turned out to be a consummate moocher, no better than his gold-digger daughter. What's that saying about the apple not falling far from the tree? I could see why Cynthia had set her sights on Ira, even with the baggage of three kids, but if Lawrence thought Mama had money stashed away from her previous husbands, he was in for a huge shock.

At least I didn't have to deal with Ira and his bratty brood this evening, just Mama, Lawrence, Lucille, and a murdered neighbor—another typical evening at Casa Pollack.

I excused myself and headed to my bedroom to rendezvous with a couple of Motrin. After gulping down the pills, I stripped off my office attire and slipped into a pair of jeans and a threadbare blue and orange Mets National League championship sweatshirt that I'd owned since the dawn of the new millennium. Glancing in the mirror at the fading logo, I wondered which would occur first—a debt-free Anastasia or a Mets World Series win. The odds for either looked equally dismal.

Even with my bedroom door closed, I continued to hear shouts of "Stupid Bolshevik!" and "Ignorant Fascist!" hurled back and forth from the living room, interspersed with an occasional squawk from Ralph. Since dinner would take at least twenty minutes to heat up, I collapsed onto my bed, drew a quilt over my body, and buried my head under a pillow to tune out the shoutfest.

If only such measures would dispel the vision of Betty Bentworth's dead body, now forever etched into my brain. As I pondered what she might have done or seen that resulted in a gaping hole where her eye used to be, I realized that after nearly two decades of living across the street from the woman, I knew next to nothing about her. Did she once have a husband? Children? A career? Did she have any living relatives? I'd never noticed anyone coming to visit her.

She rarely left her house except to attend church, run errands, do yard work, or shovel her walk in winter. Even at her advanced age, she refused to hire help of any kind. In a neighborly gesture, I once sent the boys over to dig out her property after a blizzard had dumped over a foot of snow on us. Instead of thanking them, she called the police to report trespassers on her property. So much for neighborly gestures.

~*~

The doorbell rang before my first forkful of food rendezvoused with my taste buds. "I'll get it," said Alex, jumping up from the table.

A moment later he returned with Detective Spader in tow. Nodding to me, the detective said, "Sorry to intrude on your dinner."

I'd expected the interruption. Spader had a murder to solve. For all I cared, he could set up a command center in my living room if it meant a speedier apprehension of the killer. I just wished the timing had allowed me to finish dinner first. I stood and directed Spader to follow me into the kitchen and down to the basement.

Before Karl died, I used the apartment above our garage as a studio. Once I realized that he'd gambled away all our savings, taken out a second mortgage on the house, failed to pay our taxes, and maxed out our credit cards (the trusting wife really is always the last to know,) I was forced to rent out the apartment for added income. Renting out the apartment did bring Zack into my life. However, it also meant moving my studio down to my unfinished, drafty, poorly lit basement.

I ushered Spader over to the desk and fired up my laptop to access the camera footage. Only there was no footage. "I don't understand," I said, staring at a blank screen.

Spader grunted. "I'm not surprised. We're dealing with a pro. Your neighbors' cameras were also disabled."

"Are you telling me this guy went up to every house on the block that has security cameras and disabled all of them without anyone noticing him?"

Spader shook his head. "He most likely did it remotely ahead of time."

"By hacking into the systems?"

"Exactly. It's not that hard, especially since most people don't bother to reset the password supplied by the manufacturer. The makers of these devices even post the universal password on their websites."

"But I did reset my password." Not only had Zack insisted on it, he'd made me change all my passwords to extremely complex ones that included upper and lower case letters, numbers, and symbols to increase my computer security—a different password for each site that required one.

"There are plenty of hacking programs available on the Internet," said Spader. "You just have to know where to look."

So much for security cameras—or any other form of security for that matter.

"Was anyone home here during the day?" asked Spader.

There was only one person who might have seen or heard something relevant to the case earlier that day. "Your favorite person," I said.

"You don't mean—"

"My mother-in-law."

Spader groaned.

We headed back upstairs and into the dining room. Lucille sat hunched over her plate, shoveling Kung Po chicken into her mouth. Spader planted himself alongside her chair. "Mrs. Pollack, I'd like to ask you a few questions."

Lucille continued shoveling and chewing, giving no indication that she'd heard him, let alone acknowledging his presence. Spader turned to me for assistance.

"Lucille," I said, "the detective needs to speak with you."

Around a mouthful of food she finally said, "I have nothing to say to that man."

Given Lucille's history with Spader, neither he nor I should have expected her to cooperate. "Mrs. Bentworth was murdered sometime this morning or afternoon," I said. "I'm sure the detective simply wants to know if you noticed anything out of the ordinary during the day. Isn't that right, Detective?"

"Yes, ma'am."

"So he can blame me, no doubt. Like last time."

Spader heaved a sigh. "No, ma'am. It's like your daughter-in-law said. I just want to know if you heard or saw anything unusual earlier today. An unfamiliar car parked in the neighborhood, a stranger lurking on the sidewalk, maybe."

"Never heard of anyone named Bentworth."

"She lives—lived—directly across the street," I said.

"So? Doesn't mean I ever met her." Lucille finally raised her head and glared at the detective. "I was out all day. I heard nothing; I saw nothing."

"If you do happen to remember anything—"

"I won't."

"Even if she did, she wouldn't tell you," said Mama who had remained uncommonly silent until this point. "You know how those Bolsheviks are."

Lawrence placed his hand on Mama's shoulder. "Flora, perhaps you should stay out of this. You're not helping."

She brushed his hand away. "I have a right to my opinion."

"I doubt the detective is interested in your opinion of Lucille's character."

In shock, Mama's mouth dropped open and tears sprang to her eyes. She pushed her plate aside, rose to her feet, and began to walk away from the table.

"Flora, come back," said Lawrence.

"Mama, please."

She stopped and pivoted back toward the dining room. In a quivering voice she asked, "How could you, Lawrence?"

"How could I what? Sit down and finish your dinner."

"I've lost my appetite. For both the food and you. See if you get any tonight."

"Mama!"

"Slut," said Lucille.

My sons bit down on their lips to avoid the guffaws threatening to erupt from their throats. They failed miserably. Nick, having just taken a sip of water, wound up spewing it across the table. His brother nearly gagged on a piece of pork. Even Spader found it hard to keep a straight face.

A moment later we heard a door slam. Mama had probably locked herself in the bathroom to sulk. Lawrence turned to me. "See? Talking to her only makes matters worse."

Was he blaming me? "I can't win," I muttered.

With the intensity of someone hooked on soap operas, Spader had observed the scene playing out before him, his gaze moving from one player to the next. Then again, I suppose to an outsider my life out-soaped most soap operas. He cleared his throat. "I guess I'll be going now."

"About time," said Lucille.

I rose to walk him to the door, but he waved me back into my seat. "Don't get up. I can see myself out."

~*~

Murder triggers insomnia in me. Ever since I'd walked into my cubicle nearly a year ago to discover the dead body of fashion editor Marlys Vandenburg glued to my desk chair, I've spent many a sleepless night trying to figure out whodunit and keep my family and me from becoming the killers' next victims.

I pounded my pillow into submission, trying to work off my anxiety and fear. It didn't help. I wished Zack were here. As much as I profess I can't ever again allow myself to rely on a man, all I really wanted at the moment was to have Zachary Barnes wrap his protective arms around me and whisper that everything would be all right. *Pathetic!*

My sleep-deprived state then transferred my anger to Zack. He picked a fine time to fly off to Greece or wherever he really was, doing who-knows-what for who-knows-which alphabet agency in the guise of taking pictures of what may or may not be the tomb of Alexander the Great's mother. The woman had been dead for over two millennia. Another woman, one who was alive this morning, had been murdered across the street from me. A coldblooded killer was on the loose. Damn Zack! He needed to get his priorities straight.

But then I remembered Zack knew nothing about Betty's murder. How could he? I pulled the quilts over my head and laughed hysterically at my own irrationality. Lack of sleep was definitely taking a toll on my higher brain functions.

I flung back the quilts and shoved my arms into my flannel robe and my feet into my fleece-lined slippers. Then, as I had every hour since first settling into bed, I once more quietly padded my way through the house, checking the locks on every door and window and making certain the alarm was activated. Returning to my bed, I resumed my tossing and turning.

I never had to deal with killers before my not-so-dearly-departed husband dropped dead in Las Vegas, saddling me with both debt equal to the GNP of Uzbekistan *and* his curmudgeon of a mother. You'd think that would be enough crap for one person to juggle. But no, I now have to contend with stumbling over a constant queue of dead bodies. Maybe one had nothing to do with the other, but really, how many murders does the average middle-aged suburban mom come across in a lifetime, let alone in less than a year? Can this really be coincidence?

Workplace murders are bad enough, but this time a killer had struck right across the street from my home. I doubted I'd sleep another night until the cops nabbed the guy and the justice system locked him away for life—with no chance of parole. Ever.

Cynthia's death I could understand. People hooked on drugs

often overdose. Maybe Pablo panicked and dumped her body in the canal. Maybe she wound up in the canal under other circumstances, but according to the police, she'd died of an overdose. Cocaine hadn't ended Betty Bentworth's life; an assassin's bullet had killed her. But why?

And why would someone who had taken such pains to enter Betty's home surreptitiously, leave her front door wide open? Given that everyone steered clear of Betty, months might have passed before someone discovered her body. Unless the killer wanted her body discovered. But that made even less sense than the murder itself.

Betty's mean streak almost made my mother-in-law look like Mary Sunshine. At least Lucille didn't constantly phone the police, trying to have our neighbors arrested on specious offenses. People loathed Betty. And with good reason. So maybe one of our neighbors had reached his limit. However, I'd learned enough about murder to know that when a person like Betty is killed, it's usually over some disagreement and in the heat of the moment, not an obviously planned, assassination-style execution.

As I continued to toss and turn, I kept falling back on the supposition that Betty witnessed something she wasn't supposed to see and was eliminated for that reason. But what could she possibly have witnessed on our quiet little street or during one of her weekly trips to church or the supermarket? Betty rarely left her home for any other reason.

Because Westfield lies along the main corridor between Plainfield and Elizabeth, the police routinely pull over suspect vehicles containing drug-running gang members. However, other than the occasional drug bust, we're a relatively crime-free town compared to many others in the area.

I rolled over to check the time on my nightstand clock. Two-thirty. Tossing back the quilts once more, I shoved my feet into my slippers and grabbed my robe for the fourth—or was it fifth?—time that night. Since I couldn't sleep, I decided I might as well work on my presentation for Monday.

I quietly tiptoed my way through the house, taking pains to keep from making any noise. A duet of unison snoring—one human, one canine—greeted me as I once again passed Lucille's room. Good thing I wasn't a burglar because Mephisto was certainly no watchdog. Each time I'd passed by the bedroom this evening his snore pattern remained steady.

After arriving in the kitchen without so much as the sound of ruffling feathers from Ralph, I descended the basement stairs, collected my laptop, and returned upstairs. If I was going to be up all night working, I might as well do so in the comfort of my own bed, rather than in my dank dungeon of a workroom.

I decided to make myself a cup of herbal tea before leaving the kitchen but didn't want to tempt fate with the sound of the microwave. Instead I filled the teakettle, set it on the stove to heat, then grabbed the kettle off the burner just before it began to whistle. Computer in one hand, tea in the other, I returned to the warmth of my bedroom.

Experts advise turning off computers, tablets, and e-readers two hours before bedtime to avoid sleep problems. Sound advice in theory but totally impractical for kids with homework or working moms. Besides, I was already wide-awake and had slim hope of falling asleep tonight. I might as well use the time productively.

An hour later I'd finished my baby layette presentation and emailed it to myself at work. No sleepier, even after downing a ten-ounce cup of chamomile tea, I remained on the computer. A quick Internet search revealed little in the way of recent criminal activity in town. Other than a drunk-driving arrest and a group of teens caught smoking pot behind the high school field house, nothing of significance had happened in Westfield in the past two weeks. Neither seemed a likely catalyst for Betty's murder.

Three hours remained before I needed to get ready for work. I contemplated cleaning the kitchen and bathrooms but the activity would wake Ralph, and his squawking would wake everyone else, especially Mephisto. Having no desire to walk a dog in below-freezing temperatures at three-thirty in the morning, I decided to forego any cleaning and let sleeping animals snore.

Instead, I searched online for any reference to Betty Bentworth, not that I expected to find anything of significance. Her television hailed from the last century. I doubted she owned a computer, much less had any sort of Internet presence. However, refining the search parameters, I might discover some information about her.

After nearly two decades of living across the street from the woman, I knew nothing about her other than her name. And I wasn't alone. To my knowledge none of my neighbors knew anything more than I did.

A search of "Betty Bentworth" turned up nothing. The only "Elizabeth Bentworth" I found was a reference to a woman born sometime around 1781 and listed in an 1841 census in England. I then checked nicknames for Elizabeth—Bess, Bessie, Bette, Beth, Betsy, Liz, and Lizzie—as well as less common nicknames. When nothing of significance surfaced, I searched related named, checking out Lisa, Liza, Eliza, Elle, Elsa, Elsie, Elspeth, Libby, Liddy, Lise, and Lizbeth. I even tried odd spellings I found listed on one website.

Zilch. Nada. I was just about to spend the remainder of the night playing computer solitaire when I stumbled upon a site that listed foreign forms of the name "Elizabeth." With nothing to lose, I systematically worked my way down the list of countries, pairing each given name with "Bentworth." When I typed "Belita," a Spanish derivative of Elizabeth, into the browser, the results revealed a shocking news article.

FIVE

In 1965 Belita Acosta Bentworth was arrested in Sacramento, California for attempting to kill her three young children by poisoning them with lethal doses of salt. The justice system worked much more swiftly back then, and Belita was convicted four months later. She served twenty years in a federal prison before being released in August 1985. Could Betty Bentworth be Belita Acosta Bentworth? Her age certainly fit.

I opened another window on my computer and typed Betty's address into Zillow. Her house last sold in September 1985. I certainly couldn't present this tenuous connection to Detective Spader. He'd accuse me of basing my suspicions on circumstantial evidence at best—or worse, mere coincidence. And he'd be right. I needed to dig deeper.

As daybreak began to filter into the bedroom from between the slats of my wooden blinds, I wondered: if Betty really was Belita, had one of her kids tracked her down after all these years to exact some long overdue revenge?

I glanced at the clock. Ten past six. Too early to call Detective Spader, even if I had more than speculation to offer him, but definitely time to power down my computer and start my day. Besides, before handing Spader my theory, I thought it best to check into the whereabouts of Belita's children. Were they even still alive? I knew with every hour that slipped by, the likelihood of finding Betty's killer grew slimmer. I didn't want to waste precious investigating time by sending Spader off on a wild goose chase, should he take me seriously. I'd hunt down those geese myself and present him with a platter of foie gras, when and if I located them.

~*~

Trimedia, the parent company of the magazine where I work, has a strict policy against using company computers for non-work-related activities. Nita Holzer, otherwise known as the Human Resources Attendance Nazi, not only used to write us up if we arrived a minute late to work, she also monitored our computer usage. Get caught playing *Candy Crush* or watching YouTube videos on company time, and you risked receiving a pink slip.

However, not too long ago I watched as the Morris County police escorted a handcuffed Nita Holzer and her Human Resources cohorts from the building. They currently await trial on multiple counts of embezzlement, conspiracy, theft by deception, and a variety of other charges the district attorney filed against them.

The new Human Resources employees couldn't care less about continuing Nita's Gestapo spy tactics. They're all too busy playing *Candy Crush* and watching YouTube videos. Couple that with the recent axing of our CEO, and working at *American Woman* has almost returned to the relaxed atmosphere we enjoyed before Trimedia's hostile takeover of our company. It also meant I could surf the Internet for information on Belita's children without fear of losing my job.

Upon arriving at work, I stopped first in the break room to grab a cup of coffee and snag one of two remaining blueberry pistachio muffins from the platter on the counter. Cloris keeps the break room stocked with goodies from her photo shoots and samples sent to her by vendors who want her to feature their products in our magazine. However, baked goods never last long around here. Arrive too late and you're stuck with stale chips from the vending machine.

Juggling coffee cup, muffin, purse, and tote, I headed down the corridor to my cubicle. As I slipped out of my coat, Cloris called from her cubicle across the hall. "Any more news on Cynthia's death?"

"No, but you're not going to believe what happened last night."

"Good or bad?"

An image of Betty Bentworth with a bullet hole in her head flashed before my eyes and sent a shiver skittering up and down my spine. "Bad. Really, really bad."

"Triple chocolate Crème de Cerise cupcake bad?"

"Definitely."

A moment later she darted across the hall, a cupcake in each hand. "These are too good to leave in the break room," she said, passing one to me. "I'm hoarding them for us."

Cloris's superb baking skills coupled with my slowing metabolism and lack of willpower, were slowly turning me into a female version of the Pillsbury Doughboy, but only a constant sugar rush and massive amounts of caffeine would get me through today. Besides, in gastronomic heaven chocolate and cherries ran a close second to chocolate and raspberries. I placed the blueberry pistachio muffin on my desk for later and sank my teeth into unadulterated chocolate and cherry decadence.

"Hmm. This almost makes me forget about murder," I said around a mouthful of liqueur-soaked black cherries, fudgy cake, chocolate chips, and ganache frosting. "Did you bake these?"

Cloris pulled the paper wrapper off her cupcake and licked away the frosting that clung to the wrapper edges. "Pulled an all-nighter. My motto: when you can't sleep, bake. So what happened?"

I'm betting whatever kept Cloris up last night didn't compare with the reason behind my insomnia, but I wasn't about to play the one-upmanship card with my best friend. I hate when people do that. I took a swig of coffee before speaking. "Remember that cranky old lady who lived across the street from me?"

"How can I forget? She once threatened to slash my tires if I ever parked in front of her house again."

"She's dead."

Cloris took a bite of her cupcake and shrugged. "So? She was really old, right?"

"In her eighties."

"I'll bet your neighbors are celebrating."

"Not once they learned how she died."

"Meaning?"

"She was executed."

"What!"

I told her about Betty's murder and my nocturnal research. "I think Betty was really Belita Acosta Bentworth."

"Who's Belita Acosta Bentworth?"

"A woman originally from California. She served twenty years for poisoning her children. Maybe it's all coincidence, but the timeline fits perfectly."

"You think one of her kids killed her?"

"It makes sense, doesn't it?" I filled Cloris in on what I'd learned about Belita. "When Belita was arrested in 1965, her three children ranged in age from nine months to three years. All had suffered from a variety of ailments since birth, often spending time in the hospital. Her husband, a salesman, traveled three out of five days a week. With no family in the area, care of the sickly children fell solely on Belita."

"Sounds like Munchausen by proxy."

I nodded. "Probably but no one had heard of the syndrome back then."

"Did her children survive?"

"Barely. Luckily, an emergency room doctor became suspicious when Belita brought the kids in with severe flu-like symptoms and said they'd all gotten sick at exactly the same time."

"I'm not a doctor," said Cloris, "but that would certainly raise a few red flags with me. Flu generally strikes one family member first, then travels from person to person until everyone is sick."

"The doctor thought the same thing. He ran some tests and immediately ruled out the flu. Further testing pinpointed the problem as hypernatremia."

"What's that?"

"Salt poisoning. All three kids had toxic levels of salt in their systems. When the doctor questioned Belita, she explained away the excessive levels of salt by saying she and her husband had taken the children to the beach the day before, and the kids had swallowed ocean water."

"Is that possible? Getting salt poisoning from a few mouthfuls of sea water?"

"Not according to the experts who testified at her trial. They said such high levels of sodium wouldn't even be present in near-drowning victims."

"So she force-fed them salt? Wouldn't little kids spit out or vomit up food that was too salty?"

"The district attorney claimed Belita withheld formula from the infant and fluids from the two older children. Eventually, the kids became so thirsty that they ingested the salt-laden beverages."

Cloris took another bite of her cupcake and thought for a moment. "I wonder if she was trying to gain attention and sympathy or really wanted to kill her kids."

"She certainly gained attention but no sympathy. The judge sentenced her to twenty years, speculating that her kids were probably perfectly healthy all along, that their previous ailments were also caused by their mother."

"And the father never suspected anything?"

I shrugged. "It was 1965. How many men were all that involved in childcare back then? Her husband believed what Belita told him about the kids' illnesses."

"He must have felt huge guilt afterwards. What happened to him and the kids?"

"He divorced Belita and moved out of state." I took another bite of cupcake and washed it down with a swig of coffee before continuing. "The children were probably too young to remember what their mother had done to them, but if one or more of them suffered permanent damage, at some point, they may have eventually learned the cause of their problems."

"Or knew all along. The father may not have kept the wife's crimes from their kids."

"Another possibility."

"But if your neighbor was Belita, and she was killed by one of her children, why would the kid wait so long to seek revenge?"

I had wondered the same thing and come up with a possible scenario. "Maybe they believed their mother had died when they were very young. Suppose the father recently died, and the kids first learned of their mother's crimes while cleaning out his possessions? That's how Ira wound up in my life."

Ira tracked me down after seeing a television news clip of Lucille blocking traffic with one of her Daughters of the October Revolution protests. He recognized the name from some memorabilia his father had squirreled away in the attic. That's when we discovered Ira and Dead Louse of a Spouse were half-brothers. And now I'm stuck with Ira and his brats in my life.

"You need to find out what happened to Belita's children," said Cloris.

"I know, but I ran out of time at home."

"Well, what are you waiting for?" She removed a stack of craft supply catalogues piled on the seat of the only other chair in my cubicle and deposited them on top of my file cabinet. After wheeling the chair next to the one in front of my computer, she settled into it and said, "Let's start surfing."

First I created a spreadsheet on my computer and labeled each column with Belita's name and those of her husband and children. Then I opened a browser and accessed the *Sacramento Bee* newspaper archives where I'd found all my information about the case up to this point. Under each name I jotted down everything we could find about the five family members.

John Bentworth and Belita Acosta met at the end of World War Two. Belita had worked for the International Red Cross; John was an army mechanic.

"Belita was a war bride?"

"In a manner of speaking. Her parents emigrated from Spain, but she was born in the States."

"She probably gained the medical knowledge she needed to fool people about her children's illnesses from working at the Red Cross," said Cloris.

Little information existed in the newspaper articles about the children other than their names and ages: John Jr., three; Michael, two; and Mary, nine months of age at the time of Belita's arrest.

"That would make John Jr. fifty-three, Michal fifty-two, and Mary around fifty-one," I said.

"And their father probably somewhere in his eighties."

"If he's still alive."

We uncovered one newspaper article by a reporter covering the trial that mentioned Mary experienced convulsions while in the hospital. "Convulsions can cause brain damage," I said.

"I wonder if Belita somehow continued to force salt into the kids while they were hospitalized."

"Maybe. I read up a bit on Munchausen by proxy last night. Nowadays if a hospital suspects a parent of having the syndrome, they set up surveillance cameras."

"But that's not something that would have occurred back then," said Cloris.

"No, they didn't even suspect Belita at first, even after she suggested the ocean water as a reason for the salt poisoning."

"How did they finally catch on?"

"Her husband turned her in. After the hospital diagnosed the illnesses as salt poisoning and he heard Belita's theory on how the kids got sick, he grew suspicious. He didn't remember any of the kids swallowing sea water that day. He searched his home and discovered a dozen containers of salt hidden in various locations around the house."

"Who hordes and hides salt?" asked Cloris.

"Only someone with something to hide."

"We need to find out what happened to those kids," she said. "We both have a computer. Why don't we split up? Two of us surfing will take half the time."

"Great idea. I'll take John and Mary. You search for information on John Jr. and Michael."

"Start with Facebook. Everyone is on Facebook these days."

"Everyone except me."

Cloris grinned sheepishly. "Well, actually, I'm not on Facebook, either. I hate the intrusive nature of social media. Hopefully, Belita's children don't share our sentiments."

Even though neither Cloris nor I had personal Facebook accounts, we both were tasked with posting to the site through the *American Woman* Facebook page, which gave us the ability to search Facebook for Belita's children. "We should check out the ancestry websites as well," I said.

Cloris headed back to her cubicle. A few keystrokes later I came across an obituary for John Bentworth. By now everyone else had arrived at work, and our floor bustled with activity. Not wanting anyone to overhear me, I walked across the hall to Cloris's cubicle. "John is dead."

"When?"

"Two years ago in Florida. From lung cancer. The obit says he's survived by Susan, his wife of nearly fifty years, their three children—John Jr., Michael, and Mary—and seven grandchildren. John Jr. was listed as a captain in the army. He's stationed in Guam. Michael and Mary both live in Milwaukee, or at least that's where they all were two years ago."

Cloris knit her brows together and chewed on her lower lip. "If John and Susan were married nearly fifty years, that would mean he remarried almost immediately after his divorce."

"Yeah. Makes you wonder if the traveling salesman had something going on the side."

"Maybe Belita didn't have Munchausen by proxy. If she found out John was cheating on her, she may have poisoned the kids to get back at him."

I thought about how my husband had deceived me for so many years. "If I'd discovered Karl's deceit before he died, I wouldn't have tried to kill my kids out of revenge."

Cloris laughed. "No, you would've killed Karl."

"I certainly would have fantasized about it, but I never would have acted on it."

"Because you're sane and rational. Belita wasn't. Whether she tried to kill her kids to hurt John or because she suffered from a mental disorder, she still poisoned them."

"True. But we're no closer to figuring out if Betty was really Belita. The obit states Susan was the mother of Belita's three children. Those kids were so young, they may know nothing about Belita. Have you come across anything?"

"Not yet. I couldn't find Facebook accounts for either of the boys. We might have better luck hunting down the grandchildren on social media. Do you know their names?"

"The obit didn't list them, but I'll keep digging later. I need something other than a hunch to present to Detective Spader. Right now, though, I have to prepare for a photo shoot downstairs."

"I'm caught up on work enough that I can keep surfing for a bit," said Cloris.

I headed down the hall to the closet where I stored supplies, props, and models. Our fashion and travel editors often jetted off to exotic locations for their photo shoots. My travels consisted of taking two flights downstairs to our ground floor photography studio where I also doubled as in-house stylist.

Today we were shooting the crafts for our February issue. Naomi had chosen red lace as the issue's theme, tying in to both Valentine's Day and the annual Go Red for Women heart health campaign.

For my crafts spread I had designed a series of three Victorian-inspired red monochrome crazy quilt pillows—one round, one square, and one heart-shaped. I grabbed the pillows and a cut glass vase from the closet and chose the stairs over the elevator, hoping to walk off a few of those cupcake calories. At the reception desk I stopped to pick up the roses that had been delivered for me.

"Secret admirer?" asked one of the new human resources employees as she handed over the flowers. She was younger than any of her predecessors by at least a couple of decades and decidedly better-looking. Her hair, makeup, designer outfit, and accessories suggested she spent most of her salary on her looks and wardrobe. Nonetheless, Trimedia had probably saved a bundle by hiring less experienced replacements for the four embezzlers.

Recently instituted cost-cutting initiatives had all human resources staff doubling as receptionists. The four women rotated two-hour shifts during the day. I figured it was only a matter of time before I wound up with janitorial duties added to my job description.

"I wish," I said, glancing down at the roses cradled in the crook of my elbow. "These are for today's photo shoot." I extended my hand. "I'm Anastasia Pollack, by the way. I'm one of the *American Woman* editors."

She shook my hand, offering me a friendly smile. "Ardith Callahan. Do you get to keep the flowers after the photo shoot?"

"By the time the photographer is through with them, they won't be worth keeping. The hot lights wilt them very quickly." I wasn't the only editor using the roses today. Being a third-rate magazine, we stretched our budget as far as we could.

"Too bad," she said, turning her attention back to her computer screen. I wondered if I'd interrupted a *Candy Crush* session.

Juggling pillows, vase, and roses, I continued on to the photography studio. One section of the massive room was set up to mimic a bedroom. After dumping my armload of props and pillows on a nearby table, I set about preparing for the shoot. I pulled appropriately colored linens and a comforter from the selection we kept in the studio and made the bed while the photographer set up his equipment. Then I filled the vase with water, placed the roses in the vase, set the vase on the nightstand, and arranged the pillows on the bed.

Without the need for human models, the session took less time to shoot than it had to set up. Twenty minutes later I grabbed the pillows off the bed and returned to my cubicle.

"Good. You're back," said Cloris. "I found a connection."

I dropped the pillows on my counter and darted into her cubicle. "What?"

"John Jr.'s son Trey moved to New Jersey shortly after his grandfather died."

"Why?"

"Relocation to Fort Dix."

"He's in the army, too?"

"A sergeant. He served two tours of duty in Iraq and one in Afghanistan. Now he's stateside, training recruits."

"A guy like that would know how to creep up on someone and put a bullet in her head." As far as I was concerned, I now had enough credible information to hand over to the police. "I'll call Detective Spader."

~*~

"How the hell did you find out about that?" asked Spader when I told him I thought Betty was really Belita Acosta Bentworth.

Not "where did you come up with such a crazy idea" or "your imagination is on overdrive" or even "leave the detective work to the professions, Mrs. Pollack." No, Spader had said, "How the hell did you find out about *that*?"—as if he already knew that Betty was really Belita.

I told him how I'd put two and two together with a lot of help from the Internet. "But you already know this, don't you? How?"

"We ran the vic's prints. But I'm impressed. You never cease to amaze me, Mrs. Pollack."

"I'll take that as a compliment, Detective. So do you think Belita's grandson killed her?"

"You know I can't comment on an ongoing investigation."

"Can you at least assure me that I don't have a serial killer lurking in my neighborhood?"

"I don't think you have to worry about any further murders on your street."

"Good to know, Detective. I'll let you get back to your detecting."

"Have a nice day, Mrs. Pollack." With that he hung up on me.

I crossed the corridor and told Cloris the news. "I suppose fingerprinting murder victims is standard operating procedure," she said. "Spader probably knew about Belita before you even started looking into Betty's background last night."

"At least I know my tax dollars are paying for first-class police work."

"I'm guessing Spader wouldn't tell you whether he's questioned Trey."

"Mum's the word with Spader. However, if Trey did kill his grandmother, why now?"

"Opportunity?"

"But why? All three children survived, and we haven't found evidence that any of them suffered permanent damage from the salt poisoning. I can buy into one of her kids killing her but a grandchild who never knew her? Doesn't that seem a bit of a stretch to you?"

"It does, but I'm sure we'll eventually learn Trey's motive after the police make an arrest."

"Assuming Trey is the killer."

"It seems likely, doesn't it? Anyway, for now, you can hang up your magnifying glass, Sherlock."

"With pleasure, Watson." I'd reached my quota of dead bodies for the year.

Or so I thought.

SIX

"What do you mean there's been another murder?" I stared in stunned disbelief at Spader as he stood in my foyer later that evening. He pulled a black and gray tweed knit cap off his head and shoved it into the pocket of his pea coat. "Who?"

"Carmen Cordova."

Not sweet Mrs. Cordova! My hands involuntarily clenched into two tight fists. I squeezed my eyes shut, forcing back tears as I fought to keep from pummeling the man for bringing me such horrific news. Instead, I verbally assaulted him with accusations. "You lied to me. You told me we didn't have to worry about any more murders in the neighborhood. What the hell is going on, Detective?"

"Damned if I know," he muttered. "This puts a whole new spin on the Bentworth case."

My brain shifted to Betty. "Are you saying Carmen's death eliminates any of Belita's relatives as suspects in her murder? What if the killer targeted Carmen specifically to throw you off?"

Spader cleared his throat before he spoke. "Turns out all three of Belita's kids have ironclad alibis with plenty of corroborating witnesses to back them up."

"What about the grandchildren? What about Trey?"

"Trey was testifying at a court martial for a deserter at the time of the murder."

"Alibis and witnesses can be bought."

Spader shook his head. "Don't be ridiculous, Mrs. Pollack. I personally drove down to Fort Dix this morning to question him."

"There was no way he could have driven to Westfield after he testified yesterday?"

"None. Both the court transcripts and various witnesses place him in the courtroom during the time of the murder. Trey Bentworth didn't kill his grandmother. He had no idea he even had a living grandmother."

"What about Belita's children?"

"We contacted both the military police in Guam and the Milwaukee P.D. John Jr. hasn't left the island since returning from his father's funeral two years ago."

"And Michael? Mary?"

"According to the detectives who questioned them, they were both shocked to learn Susan wasn't their real mother. Both insisted the detectives had them confused with some other Bentworths."

"I suspect Susan has a lot of explaining to do."

He shook his head. "Susan won't be explaining anything to anyone. She's in the advanced stages of Alzheimer's."

I motioned for Spader to follow me into the living room. My legs were about to turn into linguine. I needed to sit down before I collapsed onto my tiled foyer floor.

After offering Spader a seat in one of the two wing chairs

flanking the picture window, I settled onto the sofa opposite him and pulled a cable knit lap blanket off the back of the sofa and onto my lap. Suddenly I felt very cold. "How did Mrs. Cordova die?"

Carmen Cordova lived at the opposite end of the street in one of the many mid-century split-level tract homes that dotted the neighborhood. A kind woman with a gregarious personality, you could spot her from a block away by her penchant for boldly colored floral dresses. In every way Carmen Cordova was the complete opposite of the drab and dour Betty Bentworth.

"She was attacked in her home," said Spader.

"She lived alone. Who found her?"

"Her daughter. When Mrs. Cordova didn't show up for her granddaughter's birthday dinner this evening and didn't answer her phone, the daughter drove over to the house. She found her mother in the bathroom."

"Was she also shot?"

"No, she'd been stabbed multiple times."

Ralph, perched atop the bookcase, spread his wings and squawked. Spader nearly jumped out of his seat as Ralph added his Shakespearean two cents to the discussion: *It may chance cost some of us our lives, for he will stab. Henry the Fourth, Part II.* Act Two, Scene One."

"Creepy," muttered Spader, eyeing Ralph. "How's he do that?"

"Photographic memory," I answered automatically, hardly paying attention to the bird. My own mind had conjured up a graphic image of Mrs. Cordova's last moments of life. I shuddered. No one deserved such a fate. At least Betty Bentworth never knew what hit her. "Do you think she surprised a burglar?"

"Possibly. The intruder may have thought the house was empty at the time."

"I sense a *but*."

"He overlooked quite a few valuables. Of course, something may have spooked him and caused him to flee in a hurry."

"Carmen owned a lot of antique gold jewelry that looked more costume than real. He may not have realized the value of those pieces."

"That's definitely a possibility. I don't think this guy was a professional burglar."

"Why?"

"The haphazard way he ransacked the home. The items he overlooked. We're probably dealing with a drug addict hoping to score items to fence quickly. That would also explain the way Mrs. Cordova was attacked."

"What do you mean?"

"I think the killer was high at the time."

Spader's words sent a shudder coursing through my body as the implication set in. I took a deep breath and fought to keep my dinner in my stomach. "There are two killers on the loose," I whispered.

He nodded, his mouth set in a tight, grim line. "Seems that way. Bentworth's murder was a cold, calculated hit. Cordova's killer appears to have been consumed with rage toward his victim. Whether that rage was drug-induced paranoia or set off by something else is pure speculation at this point. Do you know of anyone who had a grudge against Mrs. Cordova?"

The idea seemed ludicrous to me. As much as people hated Betty, they adored Carmen. "Everyone loved her."

"Possibly not everyone."

"You think someone targeted Carmen? That this wasn't a burglary gone wrong?"

"I can't rule anything out at this time."

I shook my head. "I don't ever remember anyone in the

neighborhood having a problem with her. She was the unofficial block grandmother. She doted on her family, never had a mean word for anyone, and she made the best flan I've ever tasted."

Spader raised an eyebrow.

"Over the years she occasionally organized block parties. I think she missed the type of old-world neighborhood atmosphere of her childhood."

"Was she successful?"

"To some extent but you know how hectic life is these days—working parents, kids in extracurricular activities, the parents pulled in a million different directions all the time. People came when they could. The only person who never showed up was Mrs. Bentworth, but no one ever expected her to accept an invitation. Although, I believe Mrs. Cordova always invited her. She was that kind of woman."

"I see." Spader rose. "If you think of anything—"

I tossed aside the lap blanket and stood. "I know where to reach you, Detective."

As I accompanied Spader to the door, I asked, "You're sure there's no connection between the two murders?" I found it hard to believe we had two different killers preying on elderly residents of my small street. What were the odds?

"If there is, I'm not seeing it. Other than both victims being elderly women, nothing about the two cases matches up. The M.O.'s of the killers are completely different."

"There is one other connection that links Carmen and Betty."

"What's that?"

"They were both Latinas. Although she was born here, Betty's family came from Spain. Carmen was born in Cuba. She fled with her parents and siblings when Castro overthrew Batista's government in 1959."

"I think that's most likely just a coincidence."

"Can you be absolutely certain?"

Spader ran his hands through what was left of his hair before removing his knit cap from his pocket and pulling it over his head. "Damned if I can be certain of anything at this moment."

Not the comforting answer I wanted to hear.

Once Spader departed, I headed down the hall to tell my sons about the latest murder on our street. "I need to speak with both of you," I said, perching myself on the edge of Nick's desk.

They both pulled their noses out of their textbooks. Their faces filled with concern. "What's up?" asked Alex. When I told them about Mrs. Cordova, he said, "Jeez, Mom! It's like we're all of a sudden living in Newark or Camden."

"Or we've been sucked into some weird video game where the bad guy targets old ladies," said Nick. "What's going on? Why is someone all of a sudden gunning down people on our street?"

I didn't tell him Mrs. Cordova wasn't shot. The boys didn't need to hear the graphic details of her death. "I wish I knew," I said. "The police are baffled."

"Two old ladies on our street are killed less than a day apart," said Alex. "Doesn't that seem awfully coincidental to you, Mom?"

"Yes, it does," I said.

"The cops must be looking at some suspects, right?" asked Nick.

I shook my head. "Detective Spader had what he thought was a solid lead in Mrs. Bentworth's murder, but it didn't pan out." I paused and took a deep breath. Now for the hardest part. "He doesn't think the two deaths are connected."

"So we've got *two* killers on the loose?" asked Nick, the color draining from his face.

"Strange as it sounds, yes. Which is why I want both of you to be super careful."

"This would be a terrific time to take a vacation," said Nick.

"Yeah, if only Dad hadn't gambled away all our money," said Alex.

As if I didn't have a long enough list of items to blame on Karl Marx Pollack, I could now add placing his sons in harm's way—for the second time.

"Are you going to tell Grandmother Lucille?" asked Nick.

"My next stop," I said. "I wanted to talk to both of you first." Before leaving their room I gave each of my sons a long hug.

I found my mother-in-law in the den, *The Real Housewives of New Jersey* blaring from the television, Mephisto clutched in her arms. Ever since I'd caught Lucille and her fellow Daughters of the October Revolution watching *Dancing With the Stars* last month, she hadn't bothered to hide her obsession with reality TV.

She claimed she watched the shows for research, that she was writing a book on the detrimental effects of bourgeoisie culture on the minds of the American public, but I hadn't once seen her take any notes, let alone sit down at a computer. Instead she glued herself to the television screen, consuming a steady diet of spoiled nouveau riche housewives from various states, assorted Little People, various Amish behaving badly, and of course, all those Kardashians.

I had to take some of the blame. A few weeks ago after dealing with Ira's brats, I broke down and reinstalled basic cable. The phone company had made me an offer my kids convinced me I couldn't afford to pass up. Alex and Nick now had their ESPN back, Lucille had her Bravo and E!, and I didn't have to listen to snide remarks from Melody, Harmony, and Isaac on the state of my finances—all for the bargain price of only an additional $49.95 a month for the next two years.

Lucille ignored me when I entered the den. I had to stand in front of the television, blocking her view, in order to get her attention.

"Move," she said. "I can't see."

"Pause it. I need to speak with you."

"I'm busy." She tightened her grip on Mephisto. The poor dog whined, beseeching me with woeful eyes, as if pleading for rescue from his mistress.

"Too bad." I snatched the remote off the coffee table. Instead of pausing the show, I turned off the television. "There's something you need to know. It's important."

Mephisto yelped as Lucille leaned forward, compressing her body against his while trying to grab the remote from my hand. The poor dog finally wriggled out of her grasp, jumped off her lap, and waddled from the room.

"Manifesto, come back to mother," she called after him. When the dog ignored her, she graced me with one of her trademark scowls. "Now see what you've done! You've frightened him. The world revolves around you, doesn't it, Anastasia?"

"That's right, Lucille. It most certainly does, as evidenced by the fact that I live in the lap of luxury." I waved my arms at the decades-old, threadbare furnishings that filled my den. Everything in the room had been purchased at secondhand shops when Karl and I first married and were saving all our pennies, nickels, and dimes to buy a house. Or maybe we were only saving what he didn't gamble away. I had no way of knowing how far back in our marriage his affair with Lady Luck had started, and I never would. For all I knew, the gambling may have preceded our marriage. That part of Karl's secret life died with him.

"Get on with it then," said Lucille, crossing her arms over her sagging bosom.

I told her about Mrs. Cordova. "Perhaps you should arrange to stay with one of your friends until the police catch the killers," I said.

"You'd like that, wouldn't you? Once you get me out of the house on some trumped up excuse, you won't allow me back. I'm well aware you've been plotting a way to get rid of me from the moment I moved in."

"Lucille, two elderly women on this street are dead. You could be next."

"Not likely. I can take care of myself." She reached out her hand. "Now give me the remote. This is my son's home, and I'm not leaving."

I'm not a petty person, really. However, Lucille tries my patience to the limit, and right now I'd not only reached that limit, I'd surpassed it. By at least a mile. Instead of handing her the remote—or even placing it on the coffee table—I deliberately set it on the television console, forcing her to haul herself off the sofa and walk across the room to retrieve it. I then exited the den without a backwards glance. The woman needed to exercise more anyway. How's that for rationalizing my behavior?

I'd only made it halfway down the hall when my front door flew open, and Hurricane Flora burst inside.

SEVEN

"Anastasia! We just heard. Poor Mrs. Cordova! How did it happen?"

Lawrence followed Mama inside, closing the front door behind him but not before a flurry of dried leaves whirled their way into the foyer. Instead of bending to pick them up, he crushed several underfoot as he joined his wife. I stared down at the leaf crumbs, then up at Lawrence. "You'll find a dust pan and broom hanging in the mudroom."

Looking totally oblivious, he didn't say a word. Nor did he make any attempt to move toward the mudroom.

"Never mind about that now," said Mama. She waved her hand, swatting away the idea that her husband should be responsible for cleaning up his own mess. Why should he? She never did. At least not while she lived under my roof.

"You can sweep up later, dear," she said. "Now tell us what's going on. And what are the police doing to ensure your safety?"

Yesterday Mama and Lawrence had arrived minutes after I

discovered Betty's body and called 911. Tonight Spader had already canvassed at least part of the neighborhood before they showed up. "Listening to the wrong bandwidth tonight?" I asked Lawrence.

Lucille had definitely brought out the worst in me. I really wasn't in the mood to deal with Mama and Lawrence tonight. But at least, unlike last night, they'd arrived after dinner. I hope they didn't expect me to serve them a late night snack.

"Really, Anastasia! Where are your manners? That's no way to speak to your stepfather. We were worried about you and the boys."

When is a grown woman old enough that her mother's husbands don't count as stepfathers? I heaved a sigh. "Mama, as you can see, I'm fine. The boys are fine. You should have called."

"Well, excuse me for wanting to see for myself! Lawrence was gracious enough to drive me over here at this hour. You should appreciate that."

I closed my eyes and rattled off a quick internal count to ten. Then I backtracked. "I'm sorry, Mama. Lawrence. It's been a long day, and I've just had an altercation with Lucille—"

"I should have known that pinko had something to do with this. I raised you to have manners and respect your elders."

"Yes, Mama, you did. Now, if you don't mind, it's late, and I'm very tired. I didn't sleep last night. We can talk tomorrow." Not that I'd get any sleep tonight now that I knew we had two killers in the neighborhood. I tried to usher Mama and Lawrence toward the door, but Mama refused to budge.

"But there's a serial killer on the loose in your neighborhood! Do the police have any suspects?"

"I'm sure you know as much as I do, if not more, Mama."

"How would I know more?"

"Your husband has a police scanner, doesn't he? Isn't that how you learned about both murders?"

I wondered why it had taken them so long to show up tonight. Spader said Mrs. Cordova's daughter discovered her mother's body a little after six o'clock, shortly after I'd arrived home from work this evening. It was now close to nine o'clock. I thought about asking but given how Mama and Lawrence spend a good deal of their time together, I bit my tongue. There are some things that registered too high on my TMI barometer.

Mama choked back a sob. "But this is the second murder in two days on your street. I'm worried. Maybe you and the boys should stay somewhere else until the police catch this killer."

Killers. But I refrained from mentioning that fact. I'd never get Mama and Lawrence to leave if Mama knew two separate killers had targeted my neighbors. Instead, bad daughter that I was, I clapped my hands together and responded with sarcasm. "What a great idea, Mama! I'll book a suite at the Waldorf."

"Really, Anastasia! There's no need for sarcasm. I'm only trying to help."

"Where do you expect us to go, Mama? Should we move in with you and Lawrence?"

"Of course not. We only have one bedroom. Where would we put you and the boys?"

"Then where do you suggest we go?"

"We thought you could move in with Ira temporarily. I'm sure he wouldn't mind. He certainly has enough room for all of you."

"Ira?" I burst out laughing. *"Ira?"* Not in a million years.

"What in the world is so funny?"

"Would you like to live in the same house with Ira and his bratty kids, Mama?"

"It would only be temporary. And you'd be safe."

"One day would be a day too long. I'd rather take my chances with a couple of killers."

"Killers? *Plural?*"

Oops! "I mean killer. Two murders. I'm tired, Mama. I already told you I didn't sleep last night." Sidestepping my mother and Lawrence, I swung open the front door. Another wave of dried leaves rushed into my foyer. "I'll call you tomorrow. I promise. Please don't worry."

Mama sniffed. "Don't worry? How can I not worry? You're the only daughter I have, and the boys are my only grandchildren. Of course, I'm going to worry, but I'd worry much less if I knew you were safe at Ira's."

"Nothing is going to happen to us, Mama. Now go home. Please."

She stamped her foot. "Anastasia, as your mother I must insist. You're not only putting your own life at risk, you're risking the lives of your children."

I turned to Lawrence, who up until this point had not said a word. "Would you please help me out here?"

Lawrence wrapped his arm around Mama's shoulders. "Flora, I'm sure the police have set up patrols on the street and will be guarding all the residents. Besides, this killer seems intent on targeting elderly women. The only person in this house who has anything to worry about is Lucille."

Mama let Lawrence's words sink in for a moment. The worry lines on her forehead smoothed out, and I swear I saw her lips quirk slightly for the briefest of moments.

"That's true, isn't it?" she said, lifting her chin and gracing him with a smile. "Of course, you're right, dear. I hadn't thought of that. If anyone in this house is going to be attacked, it's that

Bolshevik pig, not Anastasia or the boys."

Mama exhaled a sigh of relief, then turned to me. "That would certainly be a huge burden off your shoulders, wouldn't it, dear?"

My mother makes no secret that she looks forward to the day she can dance on Lucille's grave. Then again, I'm sure Lucille harbors similar fantasies about Mama. The truth, though, is that Mama is correct. My life—and my financial situation—would be much less burdensome without Lucille.

However, unlike Mama, I certainly don't wish any harm to come to my mother-in-law, no matter how much of a pain in the butt she is. I just wish she lived under someone else's roof.

The front door still stood ajar. A stiff wind blew into the house along with more dead oak and maple leaves. Mama and Lawrence hadn't removed their coats, but I stood shivering in a long-sleeve T-shirt and jeans. I kissed my mother on the cheek. "Goodnight, Mama." Then I nudged her toward the door. She finally took the hint. Looping her arm through Lawrence's, she reluctantly stepped out onto the porch, turning once to look at me and sighing heavily as I closed the door behind them.

~*~

Somehow I managed to fall asleep that night, if only from sheer exhaustion. A nightmare startled me awake an hour before the alarm was set to go off. I bolted upright, my heart pounding so furiously that I thought I was having a coronary.

Slowly I became aware of my surroundings and realized a deranged psychopath wasn't hot on my heels. As my heart, pulse, and breathing slowly returned from stratospheric levels, the details of the nightmare began to fade until I remembered little more than the panic of being chased down a darkened street.

Two hours later, while sitting in the Route 287 morning rush hour creep-along, I passed the time by directing a nonstop litany of prayers heavenward. Hopefully, my prayerful efforts—along with the police still processing the most recent crime scene— would dissuade any potential murderers and keep everyone on my street safe today and every day going forward. I didn't want to come home from work tonight to find that a killer had struck down another one of neighbors.

When I arrived at work, I bypassed the break room and headed straight for Cloris's cubicle. "What the hell is going on in your neighborhood?" she asked when I caught her up on the newest murder. "Westfield is supposed to be one the safest communities in the state. All of a sudden the town's crime stats are vying with those of Newark and Camden."

"Hardly."

"Why don't the police think the two murders are connected?"

"The M.O.'s are completely different."

"You have to admit, though, it's awfully coincidental. Two elderly women murdered a day apart on the same block? What are the odds?"

"Probably too high to calculate."

"Have you thought about moving out until the killers are caught?"

"Don't you start, too." I told her about Mama's demand that I move in with Ira and his bratty brood. "I'd wind up convicted of murder. Either that or carted off in a straight jacket."

"Are his kids really that bad?"

"You have no idea." I shook my head. "No, I'll take my chances in my own home. If I thought the boys, Lucille, and I were in any danger, I wouldn't hesitate to leave, but my gut tells me we're safe."

"I hope your gut is right, Sherlock."

I sighed. "That makes two of us."

My stomach submitted its own two cents on the subject. Cloris raised an eyebrow. "Skip breakfast again?"

"Why should this day be any different from all others?"

"I dropped off two dozen raspberry duffins in the break room and made a fresh pot of coffee right before you arrived."

"Duffins?"

"The newest craze sweeping the foodie world. They're a cross between a donut and a muffin."

"First the cronut, now the duffin? Sounds like my waistline is about to expand another size."

"Not quite. Duffins are a lot less fattening, only about two hundred-fifty calories each. Cronuts are fried and run over thirteen hundred calories a piece."

I mentally calculated the number of cronuts I'd consumed since Cloris first introduced me to them last year. "Over thirteen hundred?" I groaned. "One damn cronut contained an entire day's worth of calories. No wonder I can't lose weight."

Cloris shrugged. With her metabolism she didn't have to worry how many cronuts or duffins she consumed. She never gained an ounce. Damn her! "Consider duffins a diet food," she said. "At least when compared to the cronut."

"What would I do without you?"

"Starve?"

"Probably." I left Cloris and headed for the break room to snag a duffin and a cup of caffeine before my coworkers beat me to it.

I'd just shoved the last crumbs into my mouth when my office phone rang. I quickly took a swig of coffee to wash down the duffin before answering. "Anastasia Pollack."

"It's Ardith down in reception. There's a man here to see you. Says he's your brother-in-law."

There was only one reason why Ira would show up at my

office—to strong-arm me into packing up and heading west to settle down at his McMansion until the police caught the killers. "Not gonna happen," I muttered under my breath.

"Sorry?" said Ardith. "I didn't catch that."

I sighed. "Tell him I'll be down shortly." When I heard the click on the other end of the phone, I slammed the receiver into the cradle.

"I heard that," yelled Cloris from across the hall. "Do I need to remind you of Trimedia's 'you break it, you buy it' policy?"

I crossed the hall and poked my head into her cubicle. "Do me a favor?"

She swiveled her desk chair around to face me and nodded.

"If I'm not back in ten minutes, call down to reception that I'm needed ASAP at a meeting."

Cloris raised both eyebrows. "What's with the cloak and dagger?"

"Ira's downstairs, and I have a pretty good idea why."

Cloris chuckled. "Your mother is relentless."

"Mama doesn't like not getting her way."

"Never fear. Cloris to the rescue." She glanced at her watch. "In T minus ten."

"Thanks. I owe you."

I opted for the stairwell over the elevator, figuring I might as well kill off a few of those duffin calories along the way. Although, running down two flights of stairs wouldn't come anywhere near burning off two hundred-fifty calories, I rationalized that some exercise was better than no exercise.

When I arrived at the reception desk, I found Ira schmoozing Ardith. "Has he tried to sell you a car yet?" I asked.

"I do need one," she said, "but I hate dealing with car salesman." She smiled and batted her false eyelashes at Ira. "No offense."

"None taken." He looped his arm around my shoulders and gave me a squeeze. "Anastasia will vouch for my character."

I cocked my head up toward him. "The only honest used car salesman in the country?" I asked.

"You said it." He grinned. "And I didn't even have to twist your arm."

I turned to Ardith. "If you really do need a new car, you're probably better off dealing with Ira than anyone else."

"Thanks," said Ira. He glanced down at me and grimaced. "I think." Then he reached into his suit jacket pocket, pulled out a business card and handed it to Ardith. "Call me. You won't regret it."

"What brings you all the way out to Morris County?" I asked Ira—as if I didn't know.

He took hold of my elbow and guided me across the atrium, out of earshot. "We—your mother, Lawrence, and I—believe you're not thinking rationally."

"Really?" I shrugged out of his embrace and faced him, my arms crossed in front of my chest. "Why is that?"

"You know why. You're placing yourself and your family in danger, Anastasia. I have to insist you move everyone into my house until these people are caught."

Apparently Ira had learned we were dealing with two separate killers. Mama and Lawrence probably also knew by now. I envisioned my street currently crawling with news vans and reporters knocking on doors soliciting sound bites. With any luck, they'd be gone before I returned home tonight.

I raised both eyebrows. "You insist?"

His voice filled with frustration. "Please be reasonable!"

"First, I'm not putting my family at risk. There is absolutely no indication that someone is randomly targeting people on my street."

"How can you be sure?"

"It's what the police believe."

"The police aren't always right. You more than anyone should know that."

"All the evidence supports their theories regarding both murders."

"And if their theories are wrong?"

I sighed. "Patrol cars are canvassing the neighborhood twenty-four/seven. With the police still investigating both crime scenes, my street is the safest block in the state right now—probably the entire country. Besides, the killers may never be caught. Not all murders are ever solved. You want six permanent houseguests?"

"Six?"

"Me, Alex, Nick, Lucille, Mephisto, and Ralph."

Ira shrugged. "I wouldn't mind."

"We would." Not to mention how his three juvenile delinquents would react to the invasion.

"I'm not uprooting my family just so you, Mama, and Lawrence can sleep better at night," I continued. "The commute would be a nightmare. The boys and I would have to get up before dawn to get to school and work on time, and we wouldn't arrive back at your house until eight or nine o'clock each night. I'm not putting myself or my family through that stress. We'll take our chances in our own home."

Ira threw his arms up in frustration. "But—"

"But nothing, Ira."

Across the atrium I heard the phone ring. A moment later Ardith called over to me. "You're needed upstairs for a meeting."

"I have to get back to work," I told Ira, "and I'm sure you do, too."

He grasped my upper arm a bit too tightly. "Please be reasonable. I'm worried about you."

I pried his hand from my arm, patted the top of his hand, and offered him a smile. "We'll be fine, Ira. Trust me. You know I wouldn't knowingly risk my family's well-being." Before he could answer, I pivoted on my heels and scurried down the hall to the stairwell.

Behind me, I heard him whine, "Anastasia, please!"

I raised my arm over my head and waved without turning around.

"Do you think I'm being reckless and jeopardizing my family's safety?" I asked Cloris when I returned upstairs.

"Truthfully?"

I studied the expression on her face. "You do, don't you?"

Cloris shrugged. "I don't know. I understand your reasoning, but I also understand your mother's concern."

"My mother, Lawrence, *and* Ira. They're ganging up on me with a three-pronged assault and dumping a huge guilt-trip on me." Now it looked like I could also add Cloris to that list. "What would you do if you were in my shoes?"

She didn't hesitate with her answer. "I'd do whatever was necessary to keep my kids safe."

"You don't think my kids are safe?"

"I don't know. Are you willing to take that chance?"

I sighed. "Damned if I do, damned if I don't, but there's no way I can move everyone to Ira's place, and I can't afford a hotel or temporary rental."

"If I had the room—"

I waved away the suggestion. "Thanks. I know you would if

you could, but I wouldn't impose on our friendship in that way." Still it was nice of her to offer. Not that it was really an offer, given that Cloris had downsized to help pay for her daughter's college tuition. I couldn't help laughing, though.

"What's so funny?"

"I was just picturing Alex, Nick, Lucille, and me all squeezing onto the pull-out couch in your den."

"That I'd like to see."

I headed back to my own cubicle and spent the remainder of the day mulling over my conversation with Cloris and trying not to worry about what might happen next in my neighborhood. Was I really letting my feelings about Ira jeopardize my family's safety, or was everyone else overreacting? My gut believed we were completely safe. But what if my gut was wrong? Was I willing to take that chance?

By quitting time I had reluctantly reached an unpleasant decision. If I arrived home that evening to discover more mayhem had occurred on my street, I'd pack up everyone and move to Ira's home until the killer or killers were caught. However, accomplishing such a move would necessitate bribing my sons, not to mention hogtieing Lucille because none of them would go willingly. Then, once we arrived at Ira's McMansion, I'd constantly have to sit on my hands to keep from strangling his bratty kids. Or maybe not. Lucille might club them to death with her cane before I had the chance.

I held my breath and worried my bottom lip the entire forty-minute drive home from work. While sitting in bumper-to-bumper traffic, I reached another decision: it was time to shell out money I didn't have in order to provide my sons once again with cell phones—for their safety and my peace of mind.

When I finally turned the corner onto my street, every

neuron in my body exhaled a deep sigh of relief. Not only did I find no new crime scenes anywhere in sight, but my relief increased exponentially when I saw Zack's silver Porsche Boxster parked in my driveway.

As much as recent past experience has taught me I shouldn't put my trust in, nor rely on, anyone other than myself, I have to admit I felt much safer knowing Zack had returned from his date with a dead Grecian queen's tomb. More recent deaths weighed heavily on my mind, and I knew I could count on Zack to be the voice of reason when it came to Mama's plea that I pack up everyone and move to Ira's house.

What I hadn't counted on was Mama getting to Zack before I had a chance to speak to him.

EIGHT

Zack must have been listening for my car. As I turned into the driveway, I saw his apartment door swing open. Then, in the glow of the outdoor security lights, I watched as he bolted down the steps. Before I removed the key from the ignition switch, he yanked open my driver's side door. One look at the expression on his face, and I knew he knew about the murders on the block. He confirmed this by yelling, "What the hell is going on here?"

"Nice to see you, too," I said, stepping from the car.

He shook his head once before pulling me into his arms and capturing my lips with one very long and desperate kiss.

"Who spilled the beans?" I asked when we both came up for air.

Zack continued to hold me firmly against his chest as though afraid to let go. "Your mother left a frantic voice message on my phone. I didn't see it until I switched planes in Heathrow. She said there was a serial killer loose in the neighborhood and he'd already struck twice. I tried calling. When you didn't answer, I spent the entire flight back to Newark sick with worry."

I have to admit, my heart did a little flip-flop knowing how much he cared. With Karl, I'd learned too late that I'd always played second fiddle to that very demanding and fickle mistress of his, Lady Luck.

I fished my phone out of the bottom of my purse and tried to turn it on. "The battery died." I sighed. "Yet again. The charge isn't holding for more than a few hours lately." Thanks to corporate greed, which builds planned obsolescence into every appliance and electronic gadget known to mankind, nothing lasts more than a few years these days. "I suppose I'll have to buy a new battery this weekend."

"A new battery will cost nearly as much as a new phone. You need to replace that dinosaur."

I tossed the dead diplodocus back into my purse. "I can't afford a new phone. I've already decided the boys can't go on without phones, especially now. I don't have the money for three cell phones, let alone the monthly fees."

"You can't afford not to replace your phone. It's as much a safety issue for you as it is for the boys. I'll buy you a phone."

"No, you won't."

"Yes, I will. Consider it part of my rent increase."

"I'm not raising your rent."

"Then consider it a no-interest loan, an early birthday present, a way to protect my own sanity, or all three."

"Your sanity?"

"Hell, yes. I aged ten years during that flight back from London."

I studied the firm set of his jaw. "I'm not going to win this battle, am I?"

"You're a stubborn woman, Anastasia Pollack, but in case you haven't figured it out yet, I'm an even more stubborn man. I'm buying you a new phone. End of discussion."

I mentally added a trip to the AT&T store to my already long weekend to-do list. "Why didn't you call me at the office when you couldn't reach me on my cell phone?"

"I did. The moment the plane touched down in Newark but you'd already left for the day."

"What about earlier in London?"

"No time. I raced through the terminal to make my connection. The plane literally began taxiing down the runway the moment I clicked my seatbelt. By the time I listened to Flora's message, then called your cell phone, the plane was about to take off. The flight attendant threatened to have the pilot turn the plane around and call security if I didn't power down my phone."

Given the events of the last few months, I can only imagine what was going through Zack's mind during that nearly eight-hour flight across the Atlantic. "I'm sorry I worried you. As for Mama, you do know she's prone to hyperbole."

He placed both hands alongside my cheeks, tilting my head toward his. "Are you saying there were no murders on your street?"

I bit down on my lower lip. "Not exactly."

"So there *is* a serial killer on the loose?"

"Not exactly."

He huffed out his frustration. "How about if we go inside, I pour us both a glass of wine, and you define 'not exactly'?"

"I have to make dinner. The boys will be home from soccer practice any minute."

"No, you don't. I ordered pizzas. They'll arrive in about twenty minutes. I left a note and money on the kitchen table for the boys to pay the delivery guy. You have plenty of time to explain everything to me."

"Don't count on it," I muttered under my breath. Zack shook his head again before linking the fingers of one hand through mine and leading me up the stairs to his apartment.

As I suspected, twenty minutes wasn't nearly long enough to explain the events of the last four days. Along with the two homicides on my street, I had to fill him in on Pablo's murder. I began chronologically, first catching him up on the investigation into Cynthia's death. I had just started telling him about Betty and Carmen when Nick knocked on the apartment door to announce the arrival of the pizzas.

"The police see no connection between Betty's death and Carmen's," I said as we followed Nick down the garage steps and back to the house.

"Why is that?"

"Betty was targeted. The list of people who hated her is quite long, and her killer was a pro."

"How do you know that?"

"I found her body."

"*You* found the body? Talk about burying the lede!"

I quickly explained how I came home Tuesday evening to discover Betty's front door ajar. "She was killed by a single gunshot to her eye. Given the position of her body, it was apparent the killer pointed the gun at her from the hallway, never entering the living room where she sat in the dark watching television. She never knew what hit her."

"And Carmen? Did you happen to find her body, too?"

"No. I learned about Carmen's death when Detective Spader showed up at the house last night and told me. She was probably the victim of a burglary gone wrong. I don't have many details. He said she'd been stabbed multiple times and suspects the guy was a drug addict looking for a quick score. Betty didn't suffer but poor Carmen..." I shuddered at the thought of what she must have endured the last few minutes of her life.

"So you see, we definitely don't have a serial killer targeting the neighborhood."

"No, just a hit man and a psycho burglar. What a relief!"

Wait until I told him someone had hacked into the surveillance cameras on the street. He'd toss me over his shoulder and carry me all the way to Ira's home if he had to. Maybe I'd save that topic until after a few more glasses of wine—or a far more potent potable.

I waited until Nick had stepped into the kitchen, then stopped and turned to confront Zack. "Don't you dare jump on the Mama and Ira bandwagon. Do you have any idea how difficult and complicated our lives would become if the boys and I had to commute each day from clear across the state? Not to mention you'd have to visit me in prison because there's no way I wouldn't wind up strangling his three brats."

"You'd rather put your lives in jeopardy?"

"We're not in any jeopardy! Besides, we have police protection on the street. There's a squad car parked at each end of the block."

"They didn't do such a bang-up job of protecting Carmen."

No they hadn't. I couldn't argue with that. It takes a burglar with a heck of a lot of chutzpah to target a house with a police presence on the street.

"There is one other option," said Zack, "given that I don't relish the thought of you in an orange jumpsuit."

"I'm listening."

"I move into the house until the killers are caught."

"You and Mr. Sig Sauer?" I'd recently learned Zack owned a gun after I became the victim of a stalker. He claims he needs the gun to protect himself from poachers and drug lords while on location in certain dicey areas of the globe. I saw it as yet another checkmark in the Zack as Government Agent column.

Prior to the stalking incident, I stood firmly in the anti-gun camp. Now I'm quite happy to know a kick-ass guy, who may or may not be a spy, is protecting me with his semi-automatic badass weapon. "What if you have to go out of town on assignment?"

"I'm not going anywhere until both of these guys are caught."

I threw my arms around his neck and kissed him. "Thank you for keeping me out of prison. I look ghastly in orange. You'll be amply rewarded."

"I'm counting on it."

Zack had ordered three pizzas for the five of us. Lucille had already devoured one slice of mushroom and spinach and made a serious dent into a second slice by the time we entered the dining room. Mephisto sat at her feet, gnawing on a discarded pizza crust. My sons, displaying better manners, had waited until Zack and I joined them at the table before they helped themselves to slices.

Mushroom and spinach pizza is my favorite. Lucille doesn't prefer it above pepperoni or bacon and onion, the two other pizzas on the table. Rather, she derives extreme pleasure in depriving me of my favorite toppings. Zack grabbed the box she'd commandeered and placed three slices of pizza on my plate. Then he took the remaining three slices for himself.

My mother-in-law's hostile glare spoke volumes. In a not-so-subtle way I answered her by saying, "Lucille, wasn't it nice of Zack to buy pizzas for dinner tonight?"

Ignoring me, she shoved the remainder of the mushroom and spinach slice into her mouth and reached across the table for two slices of pepperoni.

"Why bother?" asked Zack.

I sighed. "Because hope springs eternal."

The best part of dinner that evening, aside from Zack's homecoming, was not receiving a visit from Detective Spader. No further homicides had occurred on our street in the past twenty-four hours. Hopefully, the trend would continue.

Of course, that didn't prevent Mama from continuing her campaign to have us move in with Ira. She and Lawrence arrived shortly before seven o'clock. Mama strode into the dining room, took one look at Zack and said, "I hope you've talked some sense into her."

Then she headed into the kitchen. A moment later she returned with two plates, handed one to Lawrence, and the two of them proceeded to divvy up the remaining slices of pizza between them. So much for thinking I'd have one less mouth to feed once Mama and Lawrence tied the knot.

"Aren't you both lucky we had leftovers," I said. "Had I known you planned to drop by for dinner, we would have waited for you."

My sarcasm flew right over their heads. "Oh, we've already eaten," said Mama, "but it's a shame to let good pizza go to waste." She turned to Zack. "Now, Zack, dear, tell me you've convinced my stubborn daughter she needs to move in with Ira."

"What!" Lucille nearly toppled over backwards. Zack reached out to steady her chair, but she jumped to her feet, and the chair fell to the floor. "I am not moving into that man's house."

"Then stay here and get yourself killed," said Mama.

"Mama!"

"What? The woman is an idiot. If she'd rather risk death at the hands of a serial killer than accept Ira's hospitality, that's her decision."

"We're not moving in with Ira, Mama."

"No way I'm moving out there," said Alex.

"Ditto that," said Nick.

"Don't be ridiculous," said Mama. "Of course, you are. It's for your own safety. Tell them, Zachary, dear."

All eyes turned to Zack. He cleared his throat. "We've come up with a solution that doesn't involve anyone moving, Flora.

"What's that?"

"I'm moving into the house until the killers are caught."

"And what if you're targeted as well?" asked Mama. "How do you plan to keep my family safe if you're dead?" Mama turned to her husband. "Would you please help me convince them to listen to reason?"

Throughout the exchange Lawrence had concentrated on consuming a slice of pizza, never saying a word. He finished chewing, wiped his mouth on a napkin, and turned to Mama, placing his hand over hers. "Flora, you're blowing these murders completely out of proportion."

She gasped, pulling her hand away. "How can you say that when a serial killer is targeting people who live on this street?"

"There is no serial killer, Mama."

"Two people were murdered!" she shrieked two octaves above her normal voice. "Why can't any of you see what's going on here?"

"Confer with me of murder and of death," squawked Ralph from his perch atop the breakfront. *"Titus Andronicus.* Act Five, Scene Two."

Mama glared at Ralph. "Someone should murder that filthy bird. Really, Anastasia, how can you allow him in here while we're eating?" She didn't wait for me to answer. Instead she turned back to Lawrence. "Tell her she needs to move out of here."

Lawrence shook his head. "Anastasia is right. Yes, two people were murdered but in two unrelated incidents. There's no connection. No serial killer."

"Says who?"

"The police."

"You heard a discussion about the murders on your scanner?" I asked.

"I did."

"And you're willing to accept that?" asked Mama. "What if they're wrong?" She burst into tears. "I can't believe all of you! How can you do this to me?"

"This isn't about you, Mama."

"Of course it is! How could I live with myself if something happened to you and the boys?"

I never got a chance to answer Mama because at that moment someone rammed open my front door, and a dozen men dressed in SWAT gear and armed with assault rifles swarmed into my house.

NINE

Lucille screamed.

Mama gasped. All the color drained from her face. Then she fainted dead-away into a slice of half-eaten bacon and onion pizza.

"Hands behind your heads," said one of the team members.

We all complied except for Lucille who reached for her cane, which somehow hooked her plate, sending it and uneaten pizza crusts flying in the direction of the SWAT team. The next thing I knew, several SWAT members had her pinned to the floor, her hands cuffed behind her back, a gun pointed at her head.

I held my breath, waiting for Lucille to let loose a string of profanity about police brutality, but for once in her life, my mother-in-law kept her mouth shut. Ignoring the commotion, Mephisto made a beeline for one of the pizza crusts, and Ralph swooped in for another. Luckily, no one panicked and shot at either of them.

Several officers fanned out throughout the house. Intermittently they'd call out, "Clear." After several minutes they all regrouped in the living room. A moment later Detective Spader joined them.

"Nothing, sir," said the team leader.

"Stand down," he ordered. Spader glanced at Lucille's prostrate body. Her mouth set in a tight line, her one visible eye speared him with a laser-like glower. "You! I should have known you'd have something to do with this."

Spader pointed to her and said, "Release her."

This time my mother-in-law didn't hold back. "You'll be hearing from my lawyer." She proceeded to hurl every four-letter word ever invented and possibly several new ones at Detective Spader and the SWAT team. "Every single one of you," she continued. "I demand all your names."

Exhibiting more restraint than I'd ever have given him credit for, Spader remained silent while stooping to assist her to her feet. Surprisingly, Lucille didn't yell at him to take his hands off her. He then retrieved her cane and offered it to her. She snatched the cane from his hand and hurling curses in her wake, lumbered off in the direction of her bedroom.

Spader indicated to the SWAT team that they could leave, then turned to me. "My apologies, Mrs. Pollack. I'm afraid you've been the victim of a swatting."

"A what?"

"Swatting," said Zack. "It's when someone phones in an anonymous tip to the police that there's a hostage situation or a violent crime in progress."

Zack's explanation triggered a vague memory of a news story I'd heard on the radio a few months ago about such malicious pranks. The callers had targeted several high-profile Hollywood actors. However, my family and I were as far from celebrity status as Westfield, New Jersey was from Hollywood, California. "Why would someone target us?"

Spader shrugged. "Could be for any number of reasons. The practice is becoming more and more common throughout the country. We've had a spate of incidents in New Jersey over the last few months including a state assemblyman from down in Gloucester County who was swatted after he introduced legislation to toughen penalties for swatting. But we have to take these calls seriously because we have no way of knowing which are hoaxes and which are real."

"Someone could get killed," I said.

He grimaced. "It's only a matter of time."

"Why didn't you surround the house and call in a hostage negotiator if you thought we were being held captive?" I asked. I'd seen enough instances of that on the news to know such tactics were standard operating procedure in hostage cases.

"Given the recent murders on the street, we thought our best option in this case was the element of surprise," he said.

Mama had come to, thanks to Lawrence tossing half a glass of ice water on the back of her neck. She stared wide-eyed at Spader and asked, "What happened?"

"You fainted, Mama."

"I remember now. Men with guns. They swarmed into the house." She swiveled her head, her gaze darting across the room and into the living room. "Where are they?"

"Gone, dear," said Lawrence, patting her hand. "Everything is fine." He grabbed a napkin and began wiping pizza sauce from her cheek.

"Why were they here?"

Spader repeated his explanation.

"What sort of sick individual would do something like that?" she demanded.

"It's often online gamers who swat their rivals, especially if the rivals are winning." Spader turned to the boys. "Either of you participate in online gaming?"

"No, sir," said Alex.

"Same here," said Nick.

"Any problems with someone at school? Any bullying going on?"

"No," they both said in unison, shaking their heads.

Spader turned to me. "What about you, Mrs. Pollack? Have you had any problems with anyone at work?"

"No, we all get along." Well, all except for Tessa, but I doubt she has the skills to pull off such a complicated prank. Besides, as diva fashion editors go, Tessa is fairly benign compared to her predecessor. I could definitely see Marlys Vandenburg orchestrating a swatting of certain staff members, and most likely, I would have topped her hit list. But Marlys was dead, and I didn't know anyone else who hated me to the extent that she had.

"Why didn't you call first?" Mama asked Spader. "We'd have told you everyone was safe."

"Because the police would have no way of knowing whether or not someone was being coerced into saying there was no problem," said Lawrence. "They have to take every call seriously."

"That's right," said Spader. "And given the murders that occurred on the street this week, we figured this call wasn't a hoax."

"Well, thank goodness that's all it was," said Mama. She placed a shaky palm across her décolletage. "As it is, you nearly gave me a heart attack!"

For once I couldn't accuse Mama of over-dramatizing the situation. I was still waiting for my own adrenaline to descend from the stratosphere. "What happens now?" I asked Spader.

"We'll investigate, of course, but I doubt we'll turn up anything."

"Why is that?" asked Mama. "Can't you trace the call you received?"

Spader shook his head. "These guys use computers to hack into phone lines to make it appear the call is coming from the residence where the event is occurring or from a concerned neighbor. In reality, the caller is often hundreds or even thousands of miles away. The worst part is that anyone can search the Internet to learn how to swat someone. It doesn't take a computer genius to figure it out."

"So these reprobates could send you here again?" asked Mama.

"It's possible, but they usually move on to another target."

"Usually?" Mama's eyes grew wide.

"Celebrities are often the victims of multiple swattings."

Mama turned pleading eyes toward me. "A serial killer on the street isn't bad enough? Now you've got cops with guns blazing breaking into you house. You aren't safe here."

I knew nothing I said would appease Mama. She'd made up her mind. If we didn't move out of the house, one way or another, we'd all come to a gruesome end. But before I could answer her, Lucille lumbered back into the dining room.

"Where are they?" she demanded to no one in particular.

"Who?" I asked.

"All those cops." She waved a pad of paper and a pencil in the air. "I want their names and badge numbers."

And I want a month on a white sand beach in Aruba. I took a deep breath. "They've gone, Lucille."

She shoved the pad and pencil at Spader. "Write them down. All of them. Names. Badge numbers. This minute."

He placed the pad and pencil on the table. "The county police legal department will contact you with that information, ma'am."

"They'd better. That's all I've got to say."

Spader grimaced as he turned to me. "I'll make sure someone gets out here right away to fix the damage to your door, Mrs. Pollack."

As I walked him to the splintered front door, he said, "And again, I'm sorry for what happened, but you do understand we had no choice, don't you?"

"I do."

"Meanwhile, if you think of anyone who might have a beef against you or one of your kids, contact me."

I glanced over toward where Lucille still stood under the archway separating the living room from the dining room. In a voice soft enough that she wouldn't hear, I asked Spader, "Have you considered the person might be someone who has a beef with my mother-in-law?"

He scowled in Lucille's direction. "The thought definitely occurred to me. I know the Westfield police have a long list of complaints against her. We'll investigate all leads."

"And you don't think this is connected in any way to Betty's or Carmen's deaths?"

He scratched at the five o'clock shadow covering his jaw. "Anything is possible, but since the two murders don't appear connected, I fail to see how the swatting factors in to either."

"My mother insists I should pack up and leave until the killers are caught."

"I take it, you don't agree?"

"Do you?"

"I can't tell you what to do, Mrs. Pollack, but no one else on the street is panicking. If it would make you feel more comfortable, by all means, pack your bags and take a vacation. I'm certainly not ordering anyone out of their homes."

"A vacation is financially out of the question. And leaving would create a logistical nightmare for me and my kids."

However, I couldn't help but feel there are a lot of coincidences suddenly floating around. "I was willing to accept coincidence when it came to the murders, but after this swatting incident, I'm finding it hard to believe something larger isn't at play here."

Spader rubbed his jaw again. "If you can figure out how to connect the dots, Mrs. Pollack, you know where to find me. Right now I'm proceeding with the assumption that we're dealing with three separate crimes until I have proof otherwise."

He heaved a sigh. "And here I thought biding my time until retirement in Union County would be a piece of cake compared to the crime-infested streets of Newark."

~*~

It took me nearly an hour and the combined efforts of Lawrence, Zack, Alex, and Nick to convince my mother we wouldn't be murdered in our sleep that night. She didn't believe us, but she finally gave in and allowed Lawrence to take her home after a carpenter had arrived to repair my front door.

Mama tried one last parting shot as she left. With hands on hips, she stood on the front porch and declared, "I won't get a moment's sleep tonight, thanks to your stubbornness, Anastasia."

"I'll fix you a warm toddy before you go to bed," said Lawrence. "That will help you sleep." He looped his arm through hers and urged her down the walkway. Mama continued to glance over her shoulder at me as Lawrence half-dragged her toward his car.

To my shock, the carpenter handed me a bill once he finished the repairs. "This should go to the police," I said. "They broke the door."

"In the course of doing their job," he said. "The homeowner is responsible for paying for the repairs."

"But—"

He held up his hand. "Sorry, ma'am. That's the law. I accept cash, checks, and credit cards."

I stormed off to grab my checkbook, muttering a string of words that would shock my sons. "Spader breaks down my door, and I have to pay? How fair is that?" I asked Zack after the carpenter departed, check in hand.

"You of all people should know life is rarely fair."

Once my temper cooled, I slept soundly for the first time since Betty's murder on Monday, but I'm sure that had everything to do with the warm body snuggled beside me. Unfortunately, a phone call woke me the next morning an hour before the alarm was set to go off.

I glanced at the clock, groaned, then groaned again as I read the display on the Caller ID. "Good morning, Mama," I mumbled into the phone.

"Good. You're not dead. I was just checking. Maybe now I'll be able to sleep for a few hours." She hung up.

Zack rolled over as I placed the phone back in the cradle. "What did she want at this hour?"

"To make sure I was still alive."

"Thoughtful of her. Should we go back to sleep for an hour or fool around?"

I snuggled into the warmth of his body. "What do you think?"

~*~

Friday passed without any further murders, swattings, or visits from either Mama or Ira. I'm not sure Mama had given up so much as she'd gone into pout-mode. Every half hour throughout the day I received a call from her, only to have her hang up as soon as I answered and assured her I was still very much alive.

My phone's battery was draining power faster than a drought-stricken riverbed sucks up a summer rainstorm. By the sixth call that morning only fifty percent of the charge remained. Luckily, Zack had reminded me to take my charger before I left for work that morning.

"What's with all the calls?" asked Cloris. She'd been at a meeting earlier, so I hadn't had a chance to tell her about the swatting. "You don't normally receive this many calls in a week."

"Mama being Mama."

"Do I want more of an explanation than that?"

"Just her usual craziness. She's checking to make sure I'm still alive." I suppose I was lucky she'd waited until five-thirty that morning to begin her barrage of calls.

"Why wouldn't you be?"

"Bring me something chocolate, and I'll explain."

A moment later Cloris stood in the entrance to my cubicle, half a chocolate fudge brownie in her hand. "It's all I have at the moment."

I grabbed the brownie and sunk my teeth into it. Once I washed the mouthful down with a swig of tepid coffee, I caught Cloris up on the events of last evening.

"Mama in one of her moods does have an upside, though," I said.

"What's that?"

"Chances are slim she and Lawrence will drop in at dinnertime this evening."

~*~

Not only did Mama and Lawrence stay away that night, but my

evening's prospects improved even more when I arrived home to find Lucille and Mephisto nowhere in sight.

"They drove off this morning in a rusted-out circa 1960's Volkswagen minibus packed with angry-faced octogenarians," said Zack. "The driver could barely see over the steering wheel. She jumped the curb and sideswiped the oak tree at the end of the driveway."

"That would be Harriet Kleinhample and the other Daughters of the October Revolution. If we're lucky, Lucille won't return until after we've finished dinner."

As for Ira, since he didn't petition very long or very hard the day before, maybe he'd come to the realization that having me and the boys move in with him and his juvenile delinquents wasn't the best of ideas. I could only hope.

That night Alex, Nick, Zack, and I enjoyed a semi-peaceful, non-dysfunctional family dinner together, interrupted only every half hour by calls from Mama.

"What if we don't answer next time?" asked Nick after I hung up from the second call.

"Bad idea," said Alex. "She'll rush over here to make sure we're okay."

"We could leave the phone off the hook."

"She'd only call my cell phone," I said. "And if I didn't answer that, she'd call Zack. Putting up with her calls is far better than putting up with her in person right now."

"She means well," said Zack, always the voice of reason.

"I know."

The next time the phone rang, Nick answered. "We're still alive, Grandma." Then he hung up on her.

However, after a day of constant calls, Mama had succeeded in planting a seed of doubt inside my head. Was I taking the events of the last week too lightly? While the boys cleared the table, I expressed my concerns to Zack. "What if I am putting the kids and myself at risk?"

"If you feel that way, you should take Ira up on his offer."

"No one else on the street is moving out." Then again, no one else was swatted. Why would someone swat us? We weren't celebrities or gamers, and unless the boys were keeping something from me, a bully hadn't targeted either of them.

I took hold of Zack's hands. "Tell me the truth. Do you believe I'm doing the right thing by staying?"

He drew me into his arms, placed his index finger under my chin, and tilted my head up until our eyes met. "I think you need to do what you feel is best for you and the boys. If that means staying, I'm going to be right beside you."

"You and Sig?"

"Me and Sig."

I thought for a moment. "My gut tells me something odd is going on. It's all too coincidental, but I don't believe we're in any danger."

"No Spidey tingles?"

"None."

"Then go with your gut and forget about Flora's paranoia."

~*~

When the call goes out for human cloning volunteers, I plan to be first in line. As a single parent of two teenagers, I desperately need a clone, especially on the weekends when my schedule is so jam-packed that I keep a to-do list to juggle my to-do lists.

This weekend was no exception. On Saturday Nick had a JV soccer game scheduled at ten; Alex's varsity soccer game began at one. Luckily, the first was a home game, and the second was located in the adjacent town of Cranford. This allowed me just enough time to run to the supermarket between games. My other errands, including a trip to Home Depot for a toilet flushing repair kit and to the AT&T store for cell phones, would have to wait until later that afternoon.

That left leaf raking for Sunday, rain or shine because if the leaves weren't piled at the curb before the scheduled pickup on Monday, I'd have to bag them and haul them to the conservation center myself. And that was not a chore I cared to add to my to-do list.

True to his word, Zack refused to let me out of his sight, accompanying me throughout the day on Saturday. "Don't you have your own errands to run?" I asked as I froze my patootie off sitting on the soccer field aluminum bleachers.

"They can wait until during the week when you're at work."

"So you're playing bodyguard today?"

"Precisely."

"Packing heat?" I whispered softly enough that none of the other parents heard me. Zack went all stony-faced on me. "Okay, I get it. Don't ask; don't tell."

"Precisely."

"New Jersey has some of the strictest gun laws in the country. Concealed weapons permits are nearly impossible to obtain." I mentally placed another checkmark in the Zack as Government Agent column, then added under my breath, "Unless you work for an alphabet agency."

He shook his head and laughed. "You don't give up, do you?"

"I'm stubborn, remember? You said so yourself."

He wrapped his arm around my shoulders and drew me closer to him. "I also remember telling you I'm far more stubborn."

"Touché."

After watching Nick's team beat Plainfield two-zip, Zack and I headed to ShopRite. Mama called while we stood at the end of a very long checkout line.

It is a truth universally acknowledged that a single parent with too many tasks to juggle in too short an amount of time will invariably land in the checkout line where everyone in front of her is either writing a check or counting out dozens of pennies that they then proceed to drop all over the conveyer belt and floor.

In certain situations one can either go postal or put a twenty-first century spin on Jane Austen. I chose the latter, heaving a huge sigh before answering my phone. "Hello, Mama. I'm still very much alive."

"Of course you are, dear. You answered the phone."

Her voice was devoid of petulance, and she didn't hang up immediately after verifying that my heart continued to beat inside my chest. This was certainly a welcome departure from her last three-dozen phone calls. She'd either finally given in, or she wanted something. My money was on the latter.

"I need you to do me a favor," she continued.

TEN

Bingo! Did I know Mama? You bet. "What sort of favor, Mama?"

"I don't remember if I filled Catherine the Great's food and water bowls before we left this morning. Would you be a dear and run over to the condo to check for me? We won't be home until late this evening."

Great! One more item added to my already too long to-do list. "Where are you, Mama?"

"Atlantic City."

At the end of October Mama and Lawrence certainly weren't sunning themselves on the sand or wading in the ocean. The background noise told me everything I needed to know. "A casino, Mama?"

"Don't worry, dear. Lawrence isn't Karl. We're only going to play the nickel slots, and we've set a strict limit. No more than a hundred dollars each. Then we'll have dinner and take in a show."

I stared at the sweat beads forming on the packages of frozen spinach in my shopping cart. Two hundred dollars would buy two hundred boxes of store brand frozen veggies, enough to feed my family for months. Lawrence and Mama had never once offered to pay for a meal, much less bring in a pizza. Instead, they constantly dropped by unannounced and mooched off me, even though Mama knew full well the precarious state of my finances.

In addition, they'd allowed Ira to foot the bill for their wedding and honeymoon, as well as their condo. A vision of an old wine commercial swam in my head but with Lawrence taking the place of the actor who asked, *How do you think I got so rich?*

"I don't have time now, Mama. I'll run over later this afternoon."

"But Catherine the Great might be hungry and thirsty!"

"She'll survive a few hours."

"Really, Anastasia, I ask so little."

I responded by hanging up on her. A moment later my phone rang again. I glanced at the display and let the call go to voicemail, even if it meant Mama might worry I'd been gunned down on the supermarket checkout line.

"Everything okay?" asked Zack as he unloaded the contents of our cart onto the conveyor belt.

I frowned at the bags of Halloween candy he grabbed next, wondering how many of the kids who rang my doorbell Monday night would offer a thank-you. Most of them didn't even live in the neighborhood and few bothered with costumes—another reason I hated Halloween. "Hardly."

He raised both eyebrows. "Care to elaborate?"

I sighed. "Let's just say everything is status quo in Anastasia World."

"Meaning?"

"Mama needs a favor—for a change." And I was transforming into a first-class curmudgeon.

~*~

Another soccer game and the purchase of cell phones kept us busy the remainder of the afternoon. My eyes nearly bulged out of my head when the sales clerk tallied up the invoice for the three phones and the monthly plan. "It's practically a mortgage payment!"

Thanks to a summer moonlighting job, I'd recently paid off some major credit card debt I'd inherited from Dead Louse of a Spouse. Now I'd once again be carrying a balance and paying an exorbitant interest rate, but what choice did I have?

I reluctantly signed the cell phone plan agreement, then began to dig around in my purse for my wallet. Zack stayed my hand and waved his iPhone over the scanner. "No," I said. "I can't let you do that. Not all three phones."

"Too bad. It's already done."

"I'm going to pay you back."

"Someday."

"As soon as I can."

"We'll discuss it when you've climbed your way out of that financial hole Karl dropkicked you into."

Karl. Every time I thought of him and what he'd done to me and our kids, I seethed. Exactly when did the anger stage of grief dissipate? I kept waiting, but I only seemed to grow angrier as time passed.

However, without Karl's treachery, I wouldn't now have Zack in my life. Maybe every black cloud does have a silver lining. Tears sprang to my eyes. If I'd let him, I had no doubt Zack would pay off all my debts. Not that I'd ever take advantage of his generosity in that way. I fully intended to pay him back, no matter how long it took me. I squeezed his hand. "Thank you."

~*~

We sat in silence for most of the short ride home from the AT&T store. Zack kept his eyes on the road while I stared out the side passenger window. Finally he said, "I know what you're thinking."

"I don't think so."

"You're conflicted."

Okay, so maybe he could read my mind. I turned to him. "Go on, Dr. Freud."

"You don't want to become dependent on me or anyone else to solve your problems because putting your total trust in a man is what got you into this situation in the first place."

"And yet I've allowed just that, both with you and Ira." I sighed. "I'm a damned hypocrite."

"No, you're a good person thrust into difficult circumstances. There's nothing wrong with accepting help in order to survive."

"Survival is one thing, Zack; cell phones are quite another."

"Cell phones are a necessity these days, especially for someone who's morphed into Westfield's own version of Jessica Fletcher. Hell, I know law enforcement personnel who come across fewer dead bodies than you do."

I raised both eyebrows. "Exactly how many people in law enforcement do you know?"

"Enough. And it has nothing to do with you thinking I'm a spy. So let's not even go there. Instead, consider where you'd be if you didn't have a working cell phone the day Ricardo abducted you."

My cell phone had saved my life that day. If my battery had died while I was bouncing around in the locked trunk of Ricardo's Mercedes, I'd now be decomposing in an unmarked grave in the middle of nowhere. "We certainly wouldn't be sitting here having this conversation."

"Damn straight. If it helps to ease your conscience, consider the fact that I'm doing this as much for me as I am for you."

"How so?"

"I need the peace of mind of knowing that you and the boys are safe and that you have a way of getting help if you're not."

I stared at him, realizing we'd become a family, maybe not a traditional one, but a family all the same. "Did you ever expect your life would change so dramatically when you called about the apartment I had for rent?"

Zack laughed. "Life certainly works in mysterious ways, but since I now can't imagine life without you, please stop dwelling on the cost of the phones."

"I'll try."

He reached over and squeezed my hand as we turned onto our street. "Try hard."

Instead of answering, I pointed out the window. "Speaking of dead bodies, there's a car parked in Carmen's driveway, and the crime scene tape is down. I think that's her daughter Lupe's car. I should offer my condolences."

Zack continued down the street and pulled into my driveway. "Not by yourself. I'll go with you just in case you're wrong about the car."

Given that a police cruiser still sat at either end of the block, I thought Zack was being over-cautious, but I didn't argue. We stepped out of his Boxster and walked back down the street to Carmen's house.

The temperature had dipped at least fifteen degrees from earlier in the day, and the wind had picked up. The carved pumpkins that dotted the steps and porches of houses we passed had transformed from grinning and grimacing jack-o-lanterns into grotesque, deformed monsters, thanks to the squirrels that feasted on them. The few leaves that had valiantly remained clinging to branches now rained down upon us and joined the ones crunching under our feet. I glanced up at the leaden sky, covered in a skeleton of bare oaks and maples, and shivered from both the cold and the death around me—both physical and metaphysical.

Lupe answered the door when I knocked, took one look at me, and threw herself into my arms. "Oh, Anastasia!" She then burst into tears.

As a teenager Carmen's daughter Lupe often babysat for Alex and Nick when they were toddlers. Now a professional businesswoman with children of her own, she often asked one of my boys to babysit her kids.

I may have come across a plethora of murdered bodies recently, but none of them had been my own mother. I couldn't imagine Lupe's grief. I held onto her for several minutes until she'd cried herself dry. Then I guided her to a chair in the living room.

"Why would someone want to do such a horrible thing to Mami?" she asked as she swiped away at her wet cheeks. "Why couldn't he just take her jewelry and leave?"

I had no explanation for such a senseless crime other than the one Detective Spader had suggested, but I didn't think voicing that possibility would ease Lupe's anguish. So I simply shook my head.

"Do the police have any leads?" asked Zack who had met Lupe previously at one of Carmen's block parties.

"No, one of the officers suggested he might have been lying in wait for her, but that makes no sense."

Zack and I exchanged a quick glance. Spader had inferred Carmen interrupted a burglary in progress, but what if the killer only took some of Carmen's jewelry as an afterthought to make her murder appear to be a burglary gone wrong?

"Lupe," I asked, "was your mother having problems with anyone?"

"Only Batty Bentworth but everyone always has problems with her."

Except Betty was already dead when Carmen was killed. "Did something happen recently?"

Lupe nodded. "Mami was behind her in line the other day at Target. When Mrs. Bentworth went to pay for her items, she couldn't find her wallet and accused Mami of being a pickpocket."

"What happened?" I asked.

"Security detained Mami and called the police. When they arrived, one of the officers asked Mrs. Bentworth if he could check her purse to make sure she hadn't overlooked her wallet. She refused, grew defensive, and stormed out of the store."

"So this was all a stunt to cause trouble for Carmen? How typical of Betty!" How could one woman have been so unbelievably vile? She made Lucille look like Mother Theresa. If Betty weren't already dead, I'd have had to sit on my hands to keep from strangling her.

Lupe's reddened eyes grew wide, and her voice shuddered as she spoke. "You don't suppose Mrs. Bentworth had something to do with my mami's death, do you?"

"You're mother didn't tell you?"

"Tell me what?"

"Betty Bentworth died sometime Tuesday." I inhaled a deep breath and let it out slowly before adding, "Someone killed her."

All the color drained from Lupe's face. "You don't think Mami...she would never—"

I reached over and placed my hand on her knee. "Of course not. And I don't think the police believe your mother had anything to do with Betty's death, either."

"Was she robbed and killed the same way as Mami?"

"No, she was shot."

Lupe jumped to her feet. Clenching and unclenching her fists, she shook her head as she paced back and forth from the fireplace to the windows on the opposite end of the room. "That's why the detective asked me if Mami owned a gun. At the time I thought he wanted to make sure the killer hadn't stolen any weapons." She stopped pacing and turned to me. "But that's not it, is it?"

"He was conducting a thorough investigation," said Zack.

"To determine if both crimes were connected in any way," I added. "You shouldn't read too much into the question."

"No? Then why did he also ask if I owned a gun?" Her voice grew shrill and filled with panic. "He knew about the incident at Target. Does he think I'm some sort of vigilante? That *I* killed Mrs. Bentworth? I've never owned a gun in my life. Neither has Mami."

I stood and grasped Lupe's hands in mine. "Detective Spader told me he doesn't believe the murders are connected. Go home, Lupe. You shouldn't be here by yourself right now. It's too stressful for you."

"I only came for Mami's address book. I need to make sure I've notified everyone about her death, that I haven't forgotten anyone."

"Did you find the book?"

"Yes."

"Then go home. Get some sleep."

She choked out a bitter laugh. "Sleep? I can't sleep. Every time I close my eyes, I see my poor mami. It was the most gruesome thing I've ever seen, Anastasia. Like a scene right out of *Psycho*."

"What do you mean?"

"He attacked her while she was showering. I found her in the tub, the water still running." Lupe burst into tears again.

Zack and I exchanged another quick glance before I gathered Lupe up in my arms. If Carmen was in the shower, she wouldn't have known an intruder was in the house. Why didn't he simply grab her jewelry and leave?

As we fought the whipping headwinds on our walk back to the house, I posed the question to Zack.

He thought for a moment. "My guess is he was after pills. The elderly often have prescription narcotics for various ailments. He ducked into the bathroom, figuring the shower curtain would prevent Carmen from seeing him, but she heard him rifling through her medicine cabinet. If Spader's theory about the burglar being an addict is correct, maybe the guy was a meth-head or hopped up on PCP and went *Breaking Bad* crazy when she discovered him in the bathroom."

Breaking Bad. This was the second time in less than a week that someone had referenced the former TV show in regards to a gruesome murder. Why couldn't real life be more like *The Brady Bunch*?

~*~

"Crap!"

"What?" asked Zack as he fed sunflower seeds to Ralph later that evening.

"I forgot about Catherine the Great. Do we have time to make a quick stop at the condo before dinner?"

"Braaawwk!" Ralph swiveled his head to face me and flapped his wings. *"Within this hour it will be dinner-time. The Comedy of Errors. Act Two, Scene Two."*

Zack placed another sunflower seed in Ralph's open beak before glancing at his watch. "Sure but can't it wait until after dinner?"

"I was hoping we could stop at Home Depot after dinner." I explained how the toilet in the main bathroom kept running unless the boys stuck their hand in the tank and manually adjusted the rubber flapper. Of course, Lucille didn't bother. She just left the toilet running until someone else fixed it.

"Mama will have a fit if she arrives home before I've had a chance to fill Catherine the Great's food and water bowls."

"Assuming she didn't fill them herself this morning."

"True. And even if she forgot, it's not like Catherine the Great couldn't stand to lose a few pounds. Still, I'd prefer to do it now rather than run the risk of Mama arriving home while I was at the condo later. I've already dealt with too much Flora drama for one week."

Zack laughed.

"What's so funny?"

"Your idea of a romantic dinner date—plumbing supplies and cat food."

"You knew what you were getting into."

"And I wouldn't have it any other way." He drew me into his arms and kissed me in a way that made me want to jump his bones right there in the middle of the kitchen.

After enjoying the moment a bit too long, I mustered all my willpower and wiggled out of his embrace. It's one thing to have Ralph watching us, quite another to have my sons or Lucille walk in on us.

Not that I had to worry about my sons at the moment. They were in their room, totally absorbed with their new smart phones. Hopefully, they weren't going overboard texting. I had threatened them with Torquemada-style bodily harm if they exceeded the monthly data plan or spent so much as ninety-nine cents on an app.

"Dinner's ready," I called loud enough for the boys and Lucille to hear me. Then I removed a tuna casserole from the oven and a salad from the fridge, placing both on the table. Zack and I darted out the back door before anyone arrived in the kitchen.

~*~

Zack let out a whistle of surprise as I keyed in the alarm code at the condo. "That's a pretty sophisticated system for a Fanwood apartment."

"Mama hates having to deal with it, but she said Lawrence insisted on installing one. Apparently his laundry was broken into several times before he upgraded to this system. So he bought one for the condo."

Zack raised an eyebrow. "With his own money?"

"He probably finagled the cost of it out of Ira."

"I wouldn't think a commercial laundry would be a high target for burglars. It's not like they'd have lots of cash lying around."

I shrugged. "Who knows? He wants to make sure Mama is safe when he's not home. I can't argue with that."

I headed into the kitchen to check on the empress's food situation. Two empty ceramic cat bowls sat on the floor next to the French doors that opened out onto a small patio at the far end of the kitchen.

I then scoured the pantry and opened every single drawer and cupboard, unable to find a single bag, box, or can of cat food. "Where do you suppose she keeps the cat food?" I asked Zack.

Hands on hips, I scowled at the condo's sleek galley kitchen with its cherry cabinets, granite countertops, and stainless steel appliances—a far cry from my own circa 1970's kitchen of chipped Formica and cracked linoleum. "Do you suppose she ran out and forgot to buy more?"

Such a lapse would be totally out of character for Mama. Catherine the Great meant the world to her, but what if her forgetfulness was an early sign of dementia? I fought back the tears threatening to well up behind my eyes. For all her quirks and annoying habits, I loved my mother and couldn't imagine life without her. I didn't want to think about the possibility of her succumbing to any of the ravages of old age. Mama was hardly old.

Zack opened the refrigerator and removed a package of pork roll. Catherine the Great immediately jumped onto the counter and began yowling.

I frowned at the package. "I'm not frying up pork roll for Her Highness."

"It's not pork roll," he said. "It's premium cat food."

I grabbed the package out of his hand and read the label. "This has got to cost at least ten times as much as a box of Meow Mix!"

"Nothing's too good for a Russian empress," said Zack.

I went from teary-eyed over the imminent demise of my mother to wanting to strangle her faster than Zack's Porsche goes from zero to sixty. I guess my emotions showed on my face because he grabbed my shoulders with both of his hands and held fast. "Don't. She's never going to change. You know that."

"But—"

"I know."

I sighed, knowing there was no point in voicing my frustration. Mama would always be Mama, living in her own Mama world of unreality.

At that moment the doorbell rang. "Life is so freaking unfair," I muttered as I headed into the living room to answer the door.

"I'll take care of Her Highness," said Zack.

I opened the front door to find a slightly overweight man with hunched shoulders and a Yankees ball cap pulled over closely cropped salt and pepper hair. Mirrored aviator sunglasses and the upturned collar of his leather bomber jacket obscured much of his face. I fought to keep from gagging on the rancid odor of tobacco emanating from his clothes.

ELEVEN

The man kept his hands shoved in his jacket pockets as he spoke. "I'm here to see Lawrence."

I took a step back to keep from breathing in his nicotine-laced breath. "He's out for the day."

"When do you expect him back?"

"Not until later this evening."

His mouth quirked into a frown of annoyance. "I was supposed to pick something up from him."

Even though I couldn't see most of his face, something about the man seemed vaguely familiar to me. "Did we meet at the wedding?"

His cheeks shifted upward, and his nose wrinkled. Although the sunglasses hid his eyes, I had the distinct impression he was squinting at me in a lecherous, old-geezer sort of way, not that he qualified for old-geezer status. I pegged him at no more than mid-fifties. "Couldn't make it. I was out of town on a job. You his new missus?"

"Her daughter. Anastasia Pollack." I let go of the doorknob and held out my hand. "And you are?"

"Steven." He withdrew his right hand from his pocket and nearly crushed my fingers with an overly firm handshake as he stepped uninvited across the threshold.

"Steven?" I waited for a last name, but he didn't seem inclined to offer one. Undeterred, I wriggled out of his vice-like grip and asked, "Steven what?"

"Steven Jay." His head pivoted left and right as if scoping out his surroundings. "Lawrence didn't leave anything for me, did he?"

"Like what?"

"An envelope, maybe?"

"Not that I know of. We just stopped by to feed the cat. What size envelope?"

"Not sure." He approximated an inch with his thumb and forefinger. "It would be about this thick. Lots of papers. Could be a regular size business envelope. Could be one of those bigger ones, the kind that hold full sheets of paper without folding."

I glanced at the empty mail table to the side of the front door. "I'm afraid not. Would you like to leave a message for him?"

Steven shifted his weight slightly, craning his neck. He appeared to focus on something over my left shoulder. I turned to find Zack approaching from the kitchen.

"Everything okay?" he asked, coming up behind me and wrapping an arm across my shoulders.

"Yes. This is Steven Jay. He came to pick up something from Lawrence."

"An envelope," said Steven. He grabbed hold of the door and closed it behind him. "Awfully cold out there. More like December than the end of October. No point letting the heat out, right?"

"Yes, of course," I said, then added, "What sort of paperwork did you say you came for, Mr. Jay?"

"I didn't." He paused for a moment, then added, "It's business related."

"From the sale of his laundry?"

"Yeah. That. In regards to tying up some loose ends for him."

"Wait here. I'll see if there's anything sitting on his desk."

Zack stayed with Steven while I checked Lawrence's desk in the apartment's small den that also served as an office. I found only a laptop computer on the desk. No envelopes. No loose papers. The top of the file cabinet next to the desk held a tray marked *Bills to Pay* but no papers of any kind, bills or otherwise, filled the tray.

The remainder of the room held a low console with a flat-screen television opposite a small black leather sofa. There were no papers or envelopes sitting on either the console or the sofa.

I stared at the sofa, so not Mama's taste, and was reminded of her brief romance with Lou Beaumont. I wondered if she'd battled Lawrence over this sofa the way she'd fought against leather upholstery for the set of *Morning Makeovers*. If so, it appeared she'd lost this latest decorating brouhaha as well.

A moment later I returned empty-handed to the foyer.

"Nothing?" asked Steven.

"No, sorry. You'll have to come back tomorrow when Lawrence is home. He must have the papers filed away somewhere."

Steven shrugged. "Guess so. Thanks for looking." He tipped the brim of his Yankees cap toward me. "Nice meeting you, ma'am." Then he turned and headed toward a black SUV parked in front of the condo. I closed the front door. The tobacco smell remained.

"You look pissed," said Zack.

"I'm developing an extremely strong dislike toward my newest stepfather, Lawrence the Moocher."

"Don't be too quick to rush to judgment."

"What do you mean? The man recently sold a successful commercial laundry. Where's all that money? Why did Ira pay for this condo and the wedding and honeymoon?" My voice climbed several octaves as I gave way to the anger that had been growing inside me for some time. "Why am I stuck with two extra mouths to feed most nights?"

Zack placed his hands on my shoulders. "Hold on. First of all, we both know Ira has an incredible need to have people like him. He buys friendship the way most people buy weekly groceries."

I couldn't disagree with that.

Zack continued, "Besides, you only have Flora's word that Lawrence's business was successful, right?"

"True. Lawrence has never spoken about his business. I didn't even know what he did before he retired until Mama mentioned the commercial laundry facility."

"What if it wasn't successful? What if he sold the business at a loss? Or had outstanding loans that ate away at all the profit?"

"Lawrence may have lied to impress Mama." It certainly wouldn't be the first time Mama fell under the spell of a prevaricator. Lou Beaumont had her convinced he was worth millions. What he failed to mention was that he'd lost all those millions to Bernie Madoff and his Ponzi scheme.

"Or perhaps Flora heard what she wanted to hear," said Zack.

That certainly described Mama to a T. "Still, they're off gambling in Atlantic City while I'm reduced to robbing Peter to pay Paul at the end of every month." No one promised me life would always be fair, but damn, does it have to be this unfair?

Then I realized what I was doing and had been doing for days now. I hate whiners. With everything that had happened over the last few months, I'd continually fought to keep a positive attitude and not succumb to constant complaining. Karl may have kicked me down the rabbit hole into my current financial quagmire, but I refused to allow him to control me from the grave. I took a deep breath and heaved a huge sigh. "Okay, I'm going to stop whining now."

Zack quirked a smile. "Oh, were you whining? I hadn't noticed."

Before leaving the condo, I scrawled a quick note to Lawrence: *Steven Jay showed up to collect some papers from you. I suggested he come back tomorrow. A.*

~*~

The weather gods smiled down on me Sunday morning. Although the temperature hovered in the chilly mid-forties, the wind had died down, and the sun shone against a cloudless bright blue sky. "A perfect day for leaf raking," I announced as my sons entered the kitchen for breakfast.

Both Alex and Nick pulled faces as they poured themselves glasses of orange juice, but they knew better than to object. However, the same couldn't be said for my mother-in-law who had already parked herself in her chair, waiting to be served a plate of pancakes, eggs, and bacon. "I'm not raking leaves!"

"Don't worry," said Nick, taking his seat. "We wouldn't want you to break your track record by pitching in to help with something."

Lucille bristled but directed her anger toward me, not Nick. "That's what comes from your lax parenting, Anastasia. My son never would have allowed such impudence."

I had been about to reprimand Nick and insist he apologize to his grandmother, but I quickly changed my mind. Impudence aside, my son had spoken the truth. Lucille never lifted a finger around the house. Not that her physical condition would have allowed for leaf raking, but there were many other ways she could contribute if she had a mind to do so.

Communism might be her creed, but in practice she acted more like a Russian empress than a member of the proletariat. She sat on her rump, expecting everyone to wait on her.

I halted my egg scrambling, spun around from the stove, and opened my mouth, a sarcastic barb about Karl on the tip of my tongue. Zack stopped flipping pancakes and reached for my hand. Ever the voice of reason, he leaned toward me and whispered in my ear. "It's not worth it."

"I know," I muttered, returning to my egg scrambling. I closed my mouth, shut my eyes, and inhaled a deep calming breath, letting it out slowly as I fluffed the eggs.

Like Mama, Lucille would never change. Maybe I needed to take up yoga and meditation to learn how to keep both of them from burrowing under my skin.

As soon as she wolfed down her breakfast, Lucille pushed herself away from the table, grabbed her cane, and hobbled out of the kitchen, leaving her dirty dishes for someone else to rinse and place in the dishwasher.

"See what I mean," said Nick, making a face at his grandmother's departing back. "She doesn't even clear her own plate. Why do we put up with this, Mom?"

"She won't live forever," said Alex.

"Heck, she'll probably outlive us all," said Nick.

Ralph squawked and flapped his wings from atop the refrigerator where he sat observing us. *"Let not this wasp outlive, us both to sting. Titus Andronicus*, Act Two, Scene Three."

"That's enough." I waved my fork at Ralph. "From you, too."

"*Braaawk!*"

"And no heckling from the cheap seats." *Good grief!* Was I actually conversing with a parrot?

I shook my head and turned to my sons. "Lucille is a miserable old woman. We should pity her."

"Why can't she go live with one of those communist 'sisters' of hers?" asked Nick. "She cares more about them than she does us, anyway, and I'd get my room back."

"Because even they don't want her," I said.

"Huh? Aren't they her only friends?"

"It's a friendship based on a shared political philosophy. They respect her, but personally, I don't think any of them like her all that much, at least not enough to want to live with her."

"But they have a choice," said Alex. "We don't, thanks to Dad."

At one time Karl had been a good father, or at least he acted like one while he carried on his affair with Lady Luck. He spent time with his kids, reading them stories, teaching them how to ride their bikes. He became a scoutmaster when they joined Cub Scouts and coached their Little League and soccer teams. He helped them with their homework and always attended parent/teacher conferences.

Sadness settled over me at the realization that their father's deceit had shoved all those wonderful memories aside. My sons would never again think kindly of Karl. He had not only betrayed me, he'd betrayed Alex and Nick in a far worse way.

The sputtering sound of Harriet Kleinhample's antiquated orange Volkswagen minibus jumping the curb in front of the house pulled me out of my maudlin reverie. A moment later the front door slammed. "There she goes, off to foment a revolution," I said. "Did anyone walk Mephisto this morning?"

"He's her dog," said Nick.

"See if she took him with her."

Nick left the kitchen, returning a moment later with Devil Dog in tow. "Not only doesn't she help out around the house," he grumbled, "Now we're stuck taking care of her dog."

This past summer Mephisto and I had reached a détente of sorts while Lucille was confined to a rehab facility after suffering a stroke. She considered the dog's newfound affection for me a traitorous act and accused me of corrupting her pet. To punish the dog—not to mention me—she began ignoring him. Personally, I think Mephisto reveled in the lack of s'mothering attention. However, more often than not, the boys and I were now stuck walking him several times a day.

"Go grab some rakes and take your frustrations out on the leaves," I said. "Zack and I will join you as soon as we've cleaned up the kitchen and walked the dog."

We live in a neighborhood of older homes, built back during the Eisenhower era when New Jersey farmland was gobbled up by developers who replaced cornfields with countless subdivisions of mid-century modern split-levels and ranchers. Over the years the oak and maple saplings planted in yards more than half a century ago had grown to heights between seventy and a hundred feet tall. Every autumn those trees, along with the smaller flowering dogwoods, weeping cherries, and ornamental pears that dotted the neighborhood, shed a massive amount of leaves.

Both the front and back yards were ankle deep in brown, gold, burgundy, and rust colored leaves, all of which had to be deposited in a pile at the curb. After nearly three hours of raking leaves onto a tarp, then hauling the tarp to the front of the house and dumping the leaves curbside, we'd managed to make decent progress in the backyard. However, we still had several hours of work ahead of us.

I was about to suggest a coffee/hot chocolate break when Alex shouted, "Mom! Zack! Come quick!"

Zack and I rushed across the yard to where Alex and Nick had been raking leaves out of the shrubs alongside the fence that separated our yard from our next-door neighbor's yard. Alex held the handle of his rake in one hand. With his other hand he pointed to the ground where the rake's metal tines rested. Trapped within the tines, along with decaying leaves and assorted yard muck, was either an extremely lethal hunting knife or an excellent facsimile of one.

"Tell me that's a Halloween prop," I said, staring at the weapon.

Zack bent down to inspect the knife, taking care not to touch it. A dark, dry substance coated the exposed parts of the blade and much of the handle. "It's real."

"Is that blood?" asked Nick.

"Could be." He turned to me. "Did Detective Spader mention whether or not he'd recovered the weapon from Carmen's murder?"

"He didn't say. Do you think this is the knife the killer used?"

"It's certainly possible."

"What's it doing in our yard?" asked Nick.

"Good question." Zack stood up, removed the handle from Alex's grip, and gently lowered the rake to the ground. "You need to call Detective Spader," he said to me.

I motioned for the boys to step away from the rake, as if the mere presence of the knife posed a threat to us. In some ways it did, at least a threat to my carefully choreographed day of chores.

Zack confirmed this by saying, "No more raking for now. We need to leave everything as we found it until the police arrive."

Crap!

Fifteen minutes later Zack and I led Detective Spader to the spot in the backyard where the knife sat tangled in the rake. He crouched down to take a closer look. "Did anyone touch the knife?"

"No," I said. "As soon as Alex realized he'd trapped it in the rake, he called us over. Do you think it's the knife that killed Carmen?"

Spader grunted as he hefted himself upright, nearly toppling over onto his rump in the process. The man really did need to lose a significant amount of weight if he planned to reach retirement. Part of me wanted to warn him of the terminal effects of obesity, but I didn't think he'd take too kindly to my concerns over his health. I opted for discretion, keeping my tongue planted firmly in my mouth. Spader was a grown man. He had to know he was killing himself.

"We'll have to test the blood," he said after pausing for a moment to catch his breath, "but I wouldn't be surprised. What I'd like to know, though, is who have you pissed off lately, Mrs. Pollack?"

Zack stepped closer and wrapped his arm around my shoulders. "Exactly what are you inferring, Detective?"

Too shocked to speak, I stared wide-eyed at the detective.

"I'm beginning to see a pattern emerging here," he said, and I'm wondering if you might not be the central figure that connects all the dots."

TWELVE

Spader's words hit me like an ice bucket challenge during a blizzard. "Are...are you accusing me of having something to do with...with Carmen's murder? How could you—"

He held up his hand to stop my sputtering. "I'm not accusing you of anything, Mrs. Pollack."

"Then, why—?"

"I think you might know more than you realize. Hear me out."

I rattled off a quick mental count from one to ten, hoping to stay the massive amounts of fright hormones currently coursing through my body, before nodding. "Go on."

"Something about Mrs. Bentworth's door being left open doesn't sit right with me."

"This is more than just about Carmen's murder?"

Zack squeezed my shoulder. "Let him speak."

"I'm looking at the larger picture here," continued Spader. "You've got a hit man who went to great lengths to sneak into a house without being noticed. Then he exits the house through the front door, leaving it wide open. That in itself is odd."

"Or he opened the front door and left the same way he entered the house," said Zack.

"Precisely. But either way, this scenario only makes sense if—"

"If he wanted the body found," I said.

"By you," added Spader.

I gasped. "Why me? Anyone could have discovered Betty's body."

Spader raised an eyebrow. "Anyone? From speaking with your neighbors, I got the impression you're the only person on the block who would have cared enough to investigate that open door."

I pondered that for a moment and realized Spader was probably right. Everyone hated Betty. No one would care that her front door was left wide open on a chilly October evening—no one but me.

"In addition," continued Spader, "Carmen Cordova is murdered the following day, and what could very well be the murder weapon, winds up in your backyard."

"The killer needed to ditch the knife," I said. He tossed it into some bushes."

"No, he tossed it into *your* bushes, Mrs. Pollack. In your *back*yard. Not your front yard."

"Which means he either deliberately entered the yard to plant the knife—" said Zack.

"Or entered the yard next door and tossed the knife over the fence," I said. "However the knife wound up here, he went out of his way to ditch it in my yard. But why?"

"That's what we need to figure out," said Spader. "And let's not forget the swatting incident Thursday night. Someone specifically targeted this house. Three separate crimes occurred on this block within the last week, and they all lead back to you in some way."

I shook my head. "None of this makes any sense."

"It makes sense to someone," said Zack, "assuming the detective's theory is correct."

"You got a better one?" asked Spader.

"I wish I did."

"Then we'll be going with mine for now. I'm calling in the Crime Scene Unit. We're going to have to cordon off your property, Mrs. Pollack. You'll have to remain indoors while they comb through the yard."

"For how long?"

"As long as it takes."

"As in a couple of hours or an entire day?"

"As long as it takes."

Abandoning my recent vow to stop whining, I let my emotions trample my common sense. "You can't do that. We've got to get the leaves raked. The collection for our street is tomorrow."

Spader scoped out the leaves still covering a major portion of the yard and shrugged. "You can always pray for a hurricane to postpone the pickup."

If that was Spader's attempt at humor, I hoped he wasn't planning a second act on the comedy circuit once he retired. "How about if we make a deal? The knife was found in the backyard. We'll rake the front yard while you do your forensic combing through every blade of grass in the backyard."

He raised an eyebrow and scowled at me. "Really, Mrs. Pollack? I expected better from you."

And he would have received it if not for the town leaf deadline.

I offered him a weak smile and sighed in defeat. "You can't blame a girl for trying, can you?"

~*~

After lunch Zack helped me fix the toilet, a task I'd looked forward to with about as much enthusiasm as I would a case of shingles. Before Karl died he'd taken care of home repairs. For anything he couldn't fix, he'd call in a repairman. I no longer had Karl, and I couldn't afford a plumber. Luckily, Zack knew how to replace a toilet flushing mechanism because the directions on the box might as well have been written in Japanese for all the sense they made to me.

Detective Spader had allowed the boys to leave the house to watch the Giants/Eagles game at a friend's home before he cordoned off my property and posted an officer at the front of the house to keep away my curious neighbors. Meanwhile, a phalanx of police continued to comb through my yard. "I swear, they really are examining every single blade of grass," I said, watching from the kitchen window. "What else do they expect to find?"

"They won't know until they find it," said Zack.

"Meanwhile, I'll be raking leaves at midnight."

"If that's what it takes, that's what we'll do."

"There is one upside," I said.

"What's that?"

"If we're outside raking leaves after dark, no juvenile delinquents will dare TP or egg any properties on the block." For as long as I could remember the night before Halloween was known as Mischief Night, a time when teenage hellions ducked out of their homes to commit pranks and minor acts of vandalism throughout the area.

Zack tipped my chin upward and planted a peck on the tip of my nose. "I'm glad to see you've regained your positive attitude."

"Is that sarcasm?"

"From me? That's your realm of expertise. I'm just the hired gun."

"Flattery will get you everywhere."

"Good to know."

I turned away from the window. Watching the police progress was tantamount to watching grass grow. "I'll make some popcorn. Maybe there's something worth watching on television."

I pulled the popcorn maker from the cabinet above the stove and plugged it in to warm up. Zack headed for the den. Once the popcorn was popped, I joined him.

"What are you watching?"

"A PBS documentary on the mob."

"Really?" I frowned at the screen as I curled up on the couch and placed the popcorn bowl between us. "We live in New Jersey. We hear about Mafia crime on a daily basis."

I'd also had more than my share of personal run-ins with the Mafia this past winter, thanks to Karl. His loan shark had tried to shake me down for fifty thousand dollars. When that failed—because thanks to Karl, I didn't have a spare fifty dollars, let alone fifty thousand—he tried to kill me. Luckily, he failed at that, too.

They say the newest generation of Mafiosi doesn't live up to the name. Ricardo is living proof. Anyway, I had no desire to kill a few hours watching a television show about the Mafia.

Zack handed me the remote, then rose from the couch. "Find a movie."

"Where are you going?"

"This popcorn would taste a lot better with a bottle of wine."

"I don't have any. Think Spader will allow you out of the house and into your apartment?"

"I'll sweet talk him," he said, exiting the den.

I was about to commence channel surfing when an image on the screen caught my attention. I immediately hit pause and stared dumbstruck at the face partially filling the screen.

Five minutes later when Zack returned, I was still transfixed by the black and white shot of a group of men standing clustered on the sidewalk in front of the door of a pizza parlor with a large plate glass window and a striped awning.

"You shouldn't leave the screen paused too long," said Zack. "It's not good for the TV."

I waved the remote at the television. "Take a look at the guy second from the left. Remind you of anyone?" The awning had cast a shadow across the four men captured in the grainy photo, but something about one man's stance sent a shiver down my spine. "Am I letting my imagination run amok, or does that guy look like who I think it looks like?"

Zack moved closer to the television and bent down to take a better look at what appeared to be a photo taken from a security camera across the street from the pizza parlor. "Steven Jay?"

"Exactly. What's he doing pictured in a Mafia documentary?"

"Could be a coincidence."

"As in all Mafia look alike?"

Zack took the remote and pressed the Play button. The narrator began speaking about the men in the picture. "In 2009 the District Attorney believed he had an ironclad case against four high-level members of the Gambino family, pictured here in front of Mama Leone's Pizza Parlor. Vincent 'Little Vinnie' Vinci, Stevie 'Jelly Bean' Benini, Bruno 'the Nose' Labriola, and Dominic 'Macaroni' Marchioni were all charged with racketeering and extortion, but the case quickly fell apart, and all charges were dropped when a key witness disappeared and several others recanted their statements before the start of the trial."

"It's him," I said. "Steven Jay is Stevie 'Jelly Bean' Benini." That's why he looked familiar to me when he showed up at the condo yesterday. In the back of my mind I must have remembered seeing pictures of him in the newspaper and on the news during the court proceedings.

I suddenly understood why Lawrence had no money, even though he'd sold his commercial laundry concern. No wonder he sponged dinner so often. "Lawrence is being squeezed by the mob," I said. Even though I had reservations about my new stepfather, I could sympathize with his situation. I, too, had dealt with mob extortion, and I wouldn't wish that experienced on anyone, whether I disliked him or not.

"Stevie 'Jelly Bean' Benini didn't come to pick up papers from Lawrence yesterday; he came to pick up a payment."

But for what? Interest on a loan? Protection money? Lawrence no longer owned the laundry. "Do you think the mob continues to demand protection money even when a business goes out of business?" Or, like Karl, was Lawrence under the spell of Lady Luck?

"Anything is possible with the mob," said Zack. "All they care about is getting paid. However, it's more likely Lawrence is either at the mercy of a loan shark or he's being blackmailed."

"Over what?"

"There's only one way to find out. We ask him."

"Do you think he'd tell us?"

"He may not have to. We might be able to glean the truth from the way he reacts to the question."

"And then what?"

"Then we figure out what to do about it."

THIRTEEN

Spader and his crime scene investigators found no further weapons or other evidence after combing through my backyard for hours. They packed up their gear and vacated my property by five o'clock.

Zack and I finished raking the backyard as dusk transitioned into the deepening darkness of a moonless night. By the time we began tackling the front yard, our only light was the pole lamp illuminating the walkway leading to the front door and the fixture hanging above the door. We felt, rather than saw, the tree detritus under our feet. I wouldn't know the extent of our success in clearing the lawn of all the fallen leaves until daybreak.

I spent most of my raking time mulling over how Lawrence had gotten himself entangled with a member of a known crime family. "Do you suppose it has anything to do with Cynthia's drug habit?" I asked Zack. "It could explain his hardened feelings toward her."

"That's certainly a plausible supposition. Drugs and the mob go hand-in-hand."

I stopped raking the leaves at my feet and stared ahead into the night as another thought—one that caused an ominous shiver to course through my body—formed. "What if Cynthia's death was a mob hit?"

"The medical examiner ruled her death an overdose," said Zack. He, too, paused from his raking and grew thoughtful for a moment. Then he added, "Although it's possible the overdose was forced on her rather than her own doing."

As much as I had disliked Cynthia, I shuddered at how terrifying her last moments of life must have been if that were the case. No one deserved such a fate. Then I had an equally terrifying thought. "What if she was killed to teach Lawrence a lesson?" History had taught us the mob was big on administering lessons through lethal means.

And now that Cynthia was dead, were the rest of us in danger should Lawrence step out of line again? *But out of line over what?*

My throat turned dry as the Gobi. What if this was the reason for Betty and Carmen's murders and why one of the murder weapons was tossed into my bushes? Were these signs meant to frighten Lawrence? If so, what the hell was he mixed up in?

In the dim glow of the walkway lamp I looked up at Zack and realized he had had the same exact thought. "We need to get to the bottom of this," I said, "before Lawrence gets us all killed."

Or Harriet Kleinhample.

A moment later as we stood at the curb dumping another tarp full of leaves onto the pile, Harriet barreled up in her orange VW minibus and nearly drove into us. We jumped out of the way just in time.

"What are you doing standing in the street in the dark?" she demanded after she switched off the engine and slid out of the driver's seat. With hands on her hips she continued to admonish me. "You'll get yourself killed. Lucille is right. You don't have the sense you were born with, Anastasia."

She didn't wait for a response. As the rest of the packed minibus disembarked, Harriet strode like a general toward my front door. The others followed, then stood waiting while Lucille hobbled toward them, then waited some more while she fumbled in her purse for her key.

"Are you going to tell her the door is already unlocked?" asked Zack.

"I don't think so." Let her figure it out for herself. We watched as Lucille locked the door, fought with the doorknob, then finally unlocked the door and swung it open. She and her contingent then marched inside my house. The last woman to enter slammed the door behind her.

"What do you suppose they're up to?" asked Zack.

"Something that will undoubtedly annoy me, not to mention most likely cost me money."

A few months ago I arrived home to find the Daughters of the October Revolution had appropriated my printer and were running through my supply of colored ink cartridges and paper for their latest demonstration against perceived government wrongdoings. Harriet and I nearly came to blows when I unplugged the printer and grabbed it off the dining room table.

"Or maybe they just came to watch the Kardashians and raid my refrigerator," I added. Lucille was not the only member of the October Revolution addicted to reality TV. That had surprised the heck out of me.

As soon as we finished dumping the last tarp load of leaves

into the street, Zack and I cleaned off the scraps of debris clinging to nearly every square inch of our clothes and headed over to Mama and Lawrence's condo. I didn't bother telling Lucille we were leaving. I just hoped my house was in one piece when I returned. Although I didn't trust the thirteen members of the Daughters of the October Revolution alone in my home, I had no choice. They came and went as they pleased while I was at work during the week, anyway.

On the way to the condo I called the boys and told them to stay at their friend's house until we returned home. I didn't want them alone (thirteen communist octogenarians didn't count) in the house on Mischief Night—especially this Mischief Night with killers on the loose.

Alex and Nick didn't even question me. The lure of *Sunday Night Football* on a fifty-four inch flat screen TV trumped any possible curiosity on their part over why their mother would allow them to stay out so late with school the next day.

The boys were easy. Mama, on the other hand, posed a problem. "I don't want to worry her," I told Zack. "Until we know the facts, it's best to keep her in the dark. But how do we speak with Lawrence without her?" Mama would never agree to stay in one room while we confronted Lawrence in another. She'd demand to know what was going on.

"I'll talk to Lawrence after you and Flora leave the apartment."

"Leave the apartment? At this hour? Where would I take her?" The lure of a shopping trip wouldn't work. On a Sunday night neither the malls nor any of the local shops were still open.

"Go out for coffee. Tell her you need her advice on something."

"Like what?"

"Something private and female that you don't want Lawrence

to overhear."

"Are we talking pregnancy or menopause here?"

Zack shrugged. "Either would work."

I shifted in my seat to stare at his profile. "You're serious, aren't you?"

He shrugged again. "Got a better idea?"

I didn't. "I'm not going to get her hopes up about another grandchild. By first thing tomorrow morning she'll have a caterer booked."

Zack shot me a puzzled look before quickly turning his attention back to the road. "For a baby shower?"

"For our wedding."

"Oh."

"Yeah. Oh." Zack and I were nowhere near ready to move our relationship up to the matrimonial level. Or more precisely—I wasn't ready. And he knew it. Maybe at some point but for now I insisted on taking one day at a time. Unlike Mama, I didn't need a ring on my finger to feel complete. Karl's deception had done more than leave me penniless. The fallout hadn't given me cold feet; it had completely frozen my tootsies, transforming me into a consummate commitment-phobe.

However, at forty-two I was nowhere near ready to confront menopause, let alone discuss the topic with my mother, but I saw no other option. Her safety came first. If we told her the truth, we might jeopardize that safety. I blew out a sigh of frustration. "Menopause it is, then."

Zack reached over and patted my knee. "All for a good cause."

"Right."

"One other thing," said Zack.

"What's that?"

"Tell me you know how to drive a stick."

We had taken his Boxster, not having planned out our course of action ahead of time. I had learned how to drive on a standard transmission because that's what my father owned when I was seventeen years old. However, I hadn't driven a stick shift in more than two decades. Still, it had to be like riding a bike, right? Once you learn, you never forget. Or so I hoped.

"No problem," I said, forcing a massive dose of confidence into my voice—confidence I didn't feel—and hoping I fooled Zack into believing me. After offering him a radiant smile, I turned to stare out the side passenger window into the dark night. Then I closed my eyes and mentally visualized stepping on the clutch pedal with my left foot while shifting from first to second to third with my right hand. With any luck I'd avoid stripping his gears.

Luckily there were no hills between the closest all-night diner and the condo. Having to stop for a traffic light at the top of a hill would surely spiral me into a full-blown, paralytic panic attack.

We pulled up in front of the condo and walked to the front door. I paused before ringing the doorbell. I hadn't called Mama before heading over to the condo because I didn't want to risk her telling us not to come. However, barging in unannounced risked interrupting activities that fell into the TMI category. I'd already stumbled upon the randy pair too often prior to their marriage when Mama still lived with me. The images had left permanent burn scars on my eyeballs.

I held my breath as I pressed the button.

To my relief Mama, fully dressed, swung open the door within seconds. "What a lovely surprise!" she said. Sandwiching herself between us, she looped her arms with ours and led us toward the den. "Lawrence! Look who's here."

Lawrence, on the other hand, showed far less exuberance,

offering only a grunt without taking his eyes off the New York Jets and San Diego Chargers. Zack plopped next to him on the leather sofa and commenced with some ritualistic Y-chromosome bonding that included commiserating over the disappointment of a certain New York draft pick and the recent injury of a particular tight end. Neither name meant anything to me. My kids were Giants fans. As far as I knew, so was Zack, given that he spent many a Sunday watching the Giants—never the Jets—with Alex and Nick, which made his knowledge of Jets players all the more mind-boggling to me. Then again, Zack constantly amazed me.

I seized upon the opportunity, pulling Mama into the kitchen in order to be out of earshot of Lawrence. Not that he would have cared. Nothing less than an earthquake registering at least an eight on the Richter scale could have torn him from the television and even then, only had it resulted in a power outage.

However, I had to maintain my ruse. Speaking only slightly above a whisper, I said, "Mama, why don't you and I go out for a cup of coffee and some dessert while the guys watch football?"

"Why go out? And why are you whispering? I can brew up a fresh pot, and we have some brownies left over from dinner if you're hungry."

"But the diner over on Route 22 has your favorite strawberry-rhubarb pie. Besides, I have something I'd like to discuss with you in private."

Her brows knit together as she zeroed in on my belly. Then her eyes widened, and her face lit up. She clapped her hands together and bounced on the balls of her feet. "You're pregnant, aren't you? I knew it! Does Zack know? He'd better do the right thing by you."

I swear I could see the wedding planning wheels spinning behind her eyes. "I'm not pregnant."

The wheels ground to a screeching halt. The light faded from her eyes as sadness settled across her features and her shoulders sagged. She expelled one of her Drama Mama sighs. "Maybe next time."

I wrapped my arm around her shoulders and gave her a squeeze. "Mama, I'm forty-two years old, nearly forty-three. I'm way too old to go back into maternity clothes. You're just going to have to settle for the two grandchildren you already have."

"Lots of women are having babies at your age."

"Good for them, but I have no desire to join their ranks. I can barely afford the two kids I've got."

"But if you and Zack were to marry—"

"Mama!"

She twisted away from me and held up her hands in defeat. "All right. All right. What is it you want to talk about?"

"Not here."

Her eyebrows knit back together, but this time worry clouded her eyes. "All this cloak and dagger. You're not in any trouble are you?"

"Of course not. Why would you ask that?"

"Considering the last few months, can you blame me? With what you've been getting tangled up in lately—murders, kidnappings, and Lord knows whatever else you've kept from me—what am I supposed to think?"

"I'm not in any trouble."

"Then what in the world is going on? For heaven's sake, dear, spit it out already."

Hadn't I been trying to do just that? "It's a female thing, Mama. I don't want Zack or Lawrence in on the conversation."

"Well, why didn't you say so in the first place, dear?"

She grabbed her purse off the kitchen counter. As we headed

toward the front door, she called out, "Anastasia and I are off for some mother-daughter time. You boys behave yourselves."

"Enjoy," said Zack.

Mama received no response from Lawrence who was too busy cursing a Jets turnover that resulted in a San Diego touchdown.

My mother began to cross-examine me the moment the door closed behind us, but I held her off, explaining that I needed to concentrate on my driving. "I've never driven Zack's car before and haven't driven a stick shift since Dad's Mustang. Let's wait until we arrive at the diner, okay?"

"If you insist," she agreed, but curiosity overwhelmed her to the point she fidgeted the entire half-mile drive.

Other than struggling to shift the Boxster into reverse to back out of the parking spot in front of the condo, I managed to transport us to the diner without destroying Zack's transmission. Hopefully, my luck would hold for the return trip.

We found the Scotchwood Diner nearly empty and settled into a red vinyl booth toward the back. Once we had placed our orders for pie and coffee, Mama reached across the table, grabbing both of my hands in hers, and resumed her cross-examination. "Is something wrong, Anastasia? Are you ill? Have you seen a doctor?"

I pulled my hands from her vice-like grip and held them up to stop her rapid-fire questions. "I'm fine, Mama. I just wanted to know some family medical history."

"Why would you need to know family medical history if you're not concerned about something?"

I heaved a sigh. *Here goes.* "Because I think I might be entering menopause."

"Oh!"

"I don't remember you ever talking about yours."

"Well, my mother never spoke of hers, either. I just assumed you wouldn't want to hear me complaining about hot flashes and night sweats and all those other unpleasant symptoms I'd rather forget."

I was flying nearly blind here. I knew something about menopause from overhearing a few of the older women at work discuss their symptoms, but I'd paid little attention at the time. "I think I had a hot flash the other day."

"Do you have any other symptoms?"

"Like what?"

"Irritability?"

"Really, Mama? Have you not noticed the nosedive my life has taken since the winter?"

She executed an air-swat of my question, and I fixated on her perfectly manicured fingernails. I couldn't remember the last time I'd had an extra ten dollars to splurge on a manicure.

"Other than caused by the Bolshevik cow," she said.

Or by my own mother? I laughed. "Sure, ever since I learned Karl left us with debt up the wazoo."

"This is not helping, dear. How about lack of sleep?"

"Ditto. Thanks to Karl and that debt."

"Again, not helpful. What about changes in your monthly cycle?"

"None."

She reached out and patted my hand. "Then I wouldn't worry, dear. You have quite a few fertile years ahead of you."

"I'm growing irritable right now, Mama."

She feigned innocence.

"When did you start having pre-menopausal symptoms?" I asked.

"Not until my early fifties."

Our pie and coffee arrived and we tabled the conversation, eating in silence for a few minutes. I racked my brain for some way to continue the menopause conversation but came up blank. My thoughts instead turned to the real reason Zack and I had driven to the condo that night.

"Did Lawrence see the note I left for him yesterday?"

"Yes, Mr. Jay stopped by earlier today."

"He said he came for some papers that had to do with the sale of the laundry, but I didn't see anything on the mail table or on Lawrence's desk."

"I believe they were still in his file cabinet." Mama placed a forkful of pie in her mouth and closed her eyes as she savored the mixture of flaky crust and fruit. "Hmm...this was a lovely suggestion, dear. I haven't had a slice of strawberry-rhubarb pie in ages."

"I'm glad you're enjoying it, Mama. And I appreciate you setting my mind at ease about the hot flash."

Mama waved her empty fork in the air. "One hot flash means nothing. You shouldn't worry. And I believe they now call them power surges, dear."

I nodded. Of course, I knew the current lingo, but had I told Mama I experienced a power surge, she probably would have asked if it had destroyed any household appliances or electronics equipment.

I nudged the conversation back toward Steven Jay, AKA "Jelly Bean" Benini. "I didn't realize the sale of the laundry had occurred so recently."

"Not that recently. I don't remember exactly when. Lawrence mentioned it at one time." She thought for a moment. "Yes, I remember now. It was around the time Ira married Cynthia."

"Did Mr. Jay purchase the business from Lawrence?"

Mama shook her head. Before speaking, she took a sip of coffee to wash down another mouthful of pie. "No, he's our insurance agent. I believe the papers had something to do with a liability policy on the business."

Ira married Cynthia well before Karl died. Which meant Lawrence had sold his business over a year ago. Lawrence wouldn't have continued to carry liability insurance on a business he no longer owned. He would have cancelled the policy as soon as the sale went through.

Sometimes I'm glad Mama is so clueless. This was definitely one of those times. She saw nothing unusual in any of this. I, on the other hand, saw a sea of red flags whipping wildly in front of me.

I also knew beyond a doubt that no way in hell was Stevie "Jelly Bean" Benini a legitimate insurance agent.

FOURTEEN

After Mama and I finished our pie and coffee, I drove us back to the condo. Zack and Lawrence still sat glued to the television. The Jets were down 28-3. Lawrence let loose a string of expletives as the receiver fumbled and lost the ball for another turnover.

"It's only a silly game, dear," said Mama, squeezing herself into the space between Zack and her husband. She reached for the remote. "We have company. Why not turn the television off and socialize if you're so unhappy with the score?"

Lawrence snatched the remote from her hand. "Leave it!"

Mama's eyes grew wide, and her chin began to quiver. I'd had my doubts about the whirlwind courtship and marriage from the beginning, but Mama always needed a man in her life. Perhaps, had she gotten to know Lawrence better before sashaying down the aisle, she might not have taken that particular path. The previously gallant, doting Lawrence was lately proving himself anything but gallant and doting.

I've known many sports fanatics in my life but only one who

behaved in a similar fashion. At the time I thought nothing of it. Many men take their favorite sports teams too seriously and any losses too personally. At the time it never occurred to me that Karl's behavior had been a symptom of a massive gambling addiction.

The pieces started falling into place. Stevie "Jelly Bean" Benini was no insurance agent; he was Lawrence's bookie, and he'd come to collect a gambling debt. If I had an extra nickel to bet, I'd put money on it. I wondered how much Lawrence had riding on tonight's Jets/Chargers game.

I also wondered how much money, if any, Lawrence had left at this point from the sale of his business. Because I was also willing to bet my nonexistent disposable income that any profit he'd made from the sale of the business had gone right into his bookie's pockets.

"We should go," I said to Zack. "Tomorrow's a work day."

He stood and turned to Lawrence. "Maybe they'll turn things around in the second half."

"Damn well better," Lawrence muttered, not bothering to take his eyes off the screen, let alone say goodbye. Then again, he'd never said hello.

I hated leaving Mama alone with a man in such a foul mood. She slapped on a smile as she walked us to the door, but the smile didn't extend to her eyes. "Lawrence takes his sports very seriously," I said, hoping she'd drop some clue as to what was going on in her marriage.

She banished the suggestion with a wave of her hand. "You know men, dear. Sports and sex. That's all they care about. I'll get him to cheer up later."

Not wanting to hear the details of how she'd achieve that miracle, I quickly pecked her on the cheek and scurried out the door.

After we settled into the car, I asked Zack, "Did you learn anything?" A loud tummy rumble punctuated my question.

Zack raised an eyebrow as my stomach continued to insert itself in the conversation. "We never ate dinner. Just popcorn and wine earlier this afternoon. Did you eat anything at the diner?"

"A piece of pie and a cup of coffee. You?"

"Some chips and salsa but Lawrence scarfed down the lion's share. He glanced at his watch. "It's nearly ten. We should get something to eat before going home."

My stomach sounded its agreement.

Zack drove back to the Scotchwood Diner. The waitress executed a double take when she saw me reenter the diner but said nothing as she ushered us to an empty booth. We settled in and both ordered omelets, spinach and mushroom for me and bacon and cheese for Zack.

Once the waitress departed to place the order, I repeated my earlier question. "Did you learn anything from Lawrence?"

"Not much. He didn't deny Steven Jay was really 'Jelly Bean' Benini. Said he was a second cousin on his mother's side."

"Does he know Benini's a member of the Gambino crime family?"

"*Was* a member, according to Lawrence. He assured me Benini wasn't squeezing him and claimed the guy had walked away from the life after nearly going to prison a few years ago."

I raised both eyebrows and snorted. "How gullible does he think you are?" According to the documentary, Benini was a made man. There are only two ways made men leave organized crime: they either die or they enter the Witness Protection program. Even when mobsters go to prison, business continues as usual.

Zack chuckled. "He worked extremely hard at convincing me

of Benini's conversion to the straight and narrow."

"He actually carried on a conversation with you during the game?"

"No, we only spoke during the commercial breaks. The guy is a rabid fan."

And I knew why. "This is where Ralph would squawk a comment about the man protesting too much. What did you talk about the remainder of the time?"

"Nothing. He was too busy shoveling salsa and chips into his mouth in-between cursing every player and coach on the Jets."

"Do you believe him?" I sure as heck didn't. "If Benini is now such a fine, upstanding citizen, why did he use a false name when he showed up at the apartment yesterday?"

"Lawrence had an answer for that as well. Said the guy doesn't want any reminders of his past life and has legally changed his name."

I snorted again.

"Anyway," said Zack, "I led Lawrence to believe I accepted his explanation."

"Mama thinks Benini is their insurance agent." I gave Zack a recap of our conversation. "After seeing Lawrence's behavior tonight, I'm convinced Benini is Lawrence's bookie."

Zack nodded. "I came to the same conclusion after watching the way he acted this evening."

Our omelets arrived, and we ate in silence for a few minutes. When my hunger pangs finally abated, I asked, "What do we do now?"

"We call in the cavalry. I'll phone Patricia in the morning. See if she can dig up anything."

Patricia was Zack's ex-wife. From my perspective they had the friendliest divorce in the history of the world—just two people who had married way too young and for all the wrong reasons. They realized their mistake almost immediately and parted ways to lead their own lives but continued to remain friends, even after all these years. Patricia's late-in-life toddler twins by her second husband even referred to Zack as "Uncle Zackie." However, more importantly, Patricia worked as a Manhattan assistant district attorney and had access to all sorts of legal records and former cases.

But could that access prove helpful to us? "Don't you think if the D.A. had something on Benini, he'd be behind bars?"

"Probably. I'm more interested in finding out about someone else at this point."

"Lawrence?"

"Exactly."

That was the gnat that kept buzzing around my brain for the past few months. Lawrence never spoke about himself, at least not to me. From what I'd gathered, the man had also divulged very little about himself to his son-in-law or his new wife. "All we know about him is what Mama and Ira have told us."

"And that's not much."

Zack spoke around a mouthful of omelet. "I'm more concerned about whether what we know is the truth."

I certainly hoped so. For Mama's sake and for the rest of us.

~*~

My least favorite day of the year arrived with a crisp breeze and not a cloud in the sky. I had hoped for rain. Lots of it. Enough rain to keep away the hordes of Trick or Treaters that would begin ringing my doorbell well before I arrived home from work later that evening.

"I left the bags of candy on the foyer table," I told Alex and Nick before heading off to work that morning, "but don't answer the door unless Zack is here."

"Don't worry," said Nick. "We can handle pipsqueak zombies and pint-sized ninjas."

"It's not the zombies and ninjas I worry about."

As I settled in behind my steering wheel, I wished the day were already behind me. Halloween always gave me the heebie-jeebies, but this Halloween was worse than most. This year the ghosts of too many recent nightmares lurked in the shadows.

I arrived at work ten minutes before our scheduled planning meeting, just enough time to check in on Mama. No matter how much she tried to mask her sadness over her relationship with Lawrence, I saw through her false cheerfulness.

She answered on the first ring with an extremely bright "Good morning, dear!"

"You sound very chipper this morning, Mama."

"I slept like a log last night, thanks to the hot toddy Lawrence whipped up for me. Anyway, I was about to call you, dear. Lawrence booked a wine tour for us today out on Long Island. We'll be staying overnight at a bed and breakfast in Suffolk County."

"You didn't mention anything last night."

"He surprised me with it after you and Zack left, said he was going to wait until morning, but realized he'd acted a bit grouchy during the football game and wanted to apologize."

To my mind Lawrence's behavior toward Mama had gone far beyond *a bit grouchy*, but I wasn't about to argue with her. At least he'd admitted his attitude sucked and apologized.

"Would you be a dear and check in on Catherine the Great this evening?" she continued. "Make sure she has plenty of food and water to tide her over?"

Just what I needed, another line item on my to-do list but I was pleasantly surprised to hear Mama so happy after seeing her so down last night. "I'll stop in on my way home from work."

"Thank you, dear." She hung up before I could suggest she thank me with a bottle of wine. Not that I viewed our relationship as quid pro quo, but it would be nice if occasionally I didn't feel as though Mama was always taking advantage of me.

I hung up the phone, grabbed a folder from my desk, and headed for the conference room for our monthly planning meeting. Half the editors had already arrived and were helping themselves to coffee and Halloween cookies. I poured myself a cup and grabbed a mean-looking jack-o-lantern and an orange-haired witch from a box next to the coffee pot.

As soon as everyone had arrived and settled in, we first went over the status of the various issues in progress. Then Cloris, Jeanie, and I presented our suggestion of a baby theme for the next issue. Naomi loved the idea, and to our surprise Tessa didn't pitch a fit. Apparently, all the big-name designer labels now included lines for the offspring of hedge fund managers and those parents living on large trust funds.

Forget Oshkosh. The well heeled now dressed their infants and toddlers in Ralph Lauren, Oscar de la Renta, Marc Jacobs, Dolce & Gabbana, Armani, and Stella McCartney. Instead of selling his laundry business, Lawrence should have opened a chain catering to the thirty-something parents living on the Upper East Side and in Tribeca. He would have made a killing removing spit-up and pureed peas from organic cotton onesies, rompers, and pinafores.

"How many pages will you need for patterns?" Naomi asked, forcing my thoughts back to the meeting.

"It depends on how large a layette I create. I can keep the patterns simple and omit booties. They require longer directions, and never stay on babies' feet anyway."

"Knit or crochet?"

"Either. Do you have a preference?"

Naomi thought for a moment. "I have a better idea. Instead of a layette, why don't you create a couple of carriage blankets? One of each. That way we can offer a project for readers who knit and one for readers who crochet, and we won't need as many column inches for directions. We'll also be able to go with a larger photograph."

Blanket designs certainly made my life easier. Figuring out all the increasing and decreasing needed to size sweaters and bonnets correctly took an enormous amount of time. Of all the projects I created for the magazine, knitting and crochet required the most work on my part.

However, worry niggled at the edges of my brain. Having Naomi cut my editorial space before being forced to do so by additional ad placement didn't sit well with me. More importantly, it probably didn't bode well for my continued employment if I acquiesced without a fight.

I forced a smile but at the same time formulated a plan to fight for my pages. "That would work," I said, "but since we have readers of varying skill levels, why not cater to all of them from beginner to advanced?"

"Meaning?" asked Naomi.

"I can design simple blankets for beginners, ones with slightly more involved patterns for those who are more accomplished, and intricate patterns for those who enjoy a challenge."

Naomi frowned. "Six designs? How much column space will that require?"

"No more than my normal spreads." Once I gave the

directions for establishing the pattern, all the reader had to do was keep repeating it until the desired size was achieved.

Naomi nodded. "Let's compromise. Design two of each, one simple pattern and one more complex."

Not a complete victory but the best I could achieve—at least until the sales force reported in with the results of their efforts. If they had an overly successful month, two, if not three, of those four blankets would land on the chopping block.

After the other editors presented their ideas, I headed back to my cubicle to plan the blankets. I hadn't gotten very far when my phone rang. I glanced at the display and immediately recognized Detective Spader's number.

"Hello, Detective."

He got right down to business. "Mrs. Pollack, I thought you'd want to know the knife you discovered in your backyard is the weapon that killed Carmen Cordova. So I'm asking you again, are you certain there's nothing else you can tell me?"

"About what?"

"About someone who might want to make trouble for you."

"I've told you everything I know."

"You're absolutely certain? Nothing you may have forgotten or overlooked? Even a recent minor altercation with someone?"

"Honestly, Detective, I can't think of anyone other than my mother-in-law who takes pleasure in making my life miserable, but she certainly didn't kill either Betty or Carmen, and she didn't phone in a hostage threat. Were you able to pull any fingerprints from the knife?"

"None. Looks like the killer either wiped the knife before discarding it, or he wore gloves."

"Do you have any leads yet on either case?"

"You know better than to ask that, Mrs. Pollack."

I chuckled. "Someday you might slip and actually tell me something, Detective."

"Fat chance." With that parting pronouncement he hung up.

Zack had suggested that given the circumstances of Carmen's death, her killer was probably a drug addict looking for cash or pills. How likely was it that such a perpetrator would wear gloves in order to avoid leaving fingerprints? It was equally unlikely that someone like that would have the presence of mind to wipe his prints from the murder weapon before ditching it. Especially since he hadn't bothered to clean Carmen's blood from the blade. Something didn't add up. Hopefully, Spader had the same thoughts and just wasn't sharing them with me.

No sooner had I hung up from Spader, than Zack called. "I heard from Patricia."

"Already? Isn't that a little odd?"

"What's odd is that there's no record of a Lawrence Tuttnauer anywhere in the system. As far as the government is concerned, the man doesn't exist and never has."

FIFTEEN

"How can that be?"

"Good question. The only thing that makes sense is if he's in Witness Protection."

"Which makes no sense if 'Jelly Bean' Benini is his second cousin."

"Exactly."

"I'm sticking with my gambling theory and Benini is really his bookie, not his cousin."

"How do you explain there's no record of Lawrence? No birth certificate. No social security. No tax returns. No passport. Nothing."

"He's got to have a passport. He and Mama went to Paris on their honeymoon."

"Which means he used a counterfeit passport—an extremely good one in order to make it through airport security and customs without getting caught."

Fear skittered up and down my spine. Who was this man my

mother married? "Maybe Lawrence is in Witness Protection for some reason not related to the mob. Suppose he witnessed a drug deal or a murder somewhere else in the country, and the feds gave him a new identity after he testified."

"Cynthia, too?"

"It's possible, isn't it? Especially if whatever he witnessed occurred while she was still a minor."

"I suppose. I'm going to call a few other people I know and see what they can dig up."

"Alphabet people?"

"Just some people I know."

"Right. Before you hang up, I heard from Spader. The knife Alex found in the bushes is the weapon that killed Carmen."

~*~

Naomi told everyone to leave work an hour early, so we'd make it home in time to hand out candy to the little costumed beggars anxiously ringing our doorbells and hoping for the 'good stuff,' rather than generic, cellophane-wrapped lollipops. I didn't begrudge the younger neighborhood kids their yearly candy extortion. What transformed me into a curmudgeon were the teenagers who didn't even bother to don costumes and the families from less affluent towns who drove their kids to Westfield to score better bounty.

Westfield might have a reputation for being an upscale community, but not all of us worked on Wall Street or at high-power New York law firms. I could rattle off dozens of better uses for that twenty dollars I dropped on chocolate bars at ShopRite the other day.

Even leaving work an hour early, I hit traffic on Rt. 78 and slowed to a fifteen-mile-an-hour crawl east of Warren. I turned on the news, hoping for a traffic report. Instead, I heard the ominous musical notes that signaled a breaking news story. The serious voice of a female reporter followed.

"The body of Stevie 'Jelly Bean' Benini, a reputed, high-ranking member of the Gambino crime family, was discovered about an hour ago slumped behind the wheel of a late model black Escalade parked on a residential section of JFK Boulevard in Weehawken."

Startled, I wasn't paying attention to traffic and didn't realize the car in front of me had stopped. I slammed on the brakes, stopping inches from his back bumper. Brakes squealed behind me, followed by a series of irate horn blasts. I glanced in my rearview mirror in time to see the driver of one of those enormous macho pickup trucks shooting me the bird. Ignoring him, I reached for the radio knob and cranked up the volume.

"Initial reports indicate Benini died of natural causes, but the medical examiner will perform an autopsy to determine cause of death.

"In 2009 Benini was indicted, along with several others, on charges of racketeering and extortion. Shortly before the case went to trial, the DA was forced to drop all charges after their star witness disappeared, and several others scheduled to testify recanted their initial statements to investigators, claiming the detectives had used excessive force to coerce those statements from them."

The historical information parroted that of the documentary Zack and I had watched. The report ended without offering any further facts, and the station segued to a commercial break.

Had 'Jelly Bean' Benini really died of natural causes? My Spidey senses told me otherwise. More importantly, did his death have anything to do with Lawrence? I sure as hell hoped not, but Lawrence had connections to 'Jelly Bean,' and he'd definitely lied about the nature of those ties.

I fished my phone out of my purse and placed a call to Zack. When he answered, I dispensed with pleasantries and greeted him by asking, "Did you hear the news about 'Jelly Bean'?"

"Just now. Where are you?"

"Stuck in traffic on my way home, but I've got to stop at the condo first." I explained why. "Looks like the lovebirds are back to being all lovey-dovey."

"Good. Better for Flora that way. Get back here as soon as you can. On second thought, forget about the feline empress for now. I'll go over there with you later tonight after all the doorbell ringing ends."

"No need. I only have to check to make sure she still has food and water. I'll be in and out in under five minutes."

I hung up from Zack and decided to ditch the highway for the back roads, exiting at the next off ramp. Twenty minutes later I pulled up in front of the condo, keyed in the alarm code, and let myself into the apartment.

Catherine the Great sat sunning herself in front of the French doors that led to the small back patio. She glanced my way, then turned her face back to the setting sun, having decided I wasn't worth the effort of further exertion on her part, much less a royal greeting. After all, I was but a mere servant. I retrieved her pricey cat food from the fridge, adding some to her empty food bowl, and topped off her water dish.

I was about to leave the apartment when the urge to snoop in Lawrence's file cabinet drew me to the den. I quickly discovered the file cabinet was locked. A standard metal two-drawer unit, it contained a simple locking mechanism in one corner above the top drawer. Never having picked a lock in my life, I had no idea how long it would take or even if I'd succeed, but I knew I could find instructions on the Internet.

I flipped up the lid of the laptop sitting on the desk and hit the power button. A minute later I frowned at the screen. Damn! The computer was password protected. However, now that I owned a brand new smart phone, I had another way of accessing the Internet. Less than a minute later I was watching a Youtube tutorial on lock picking.

I grabbed two paper clips from the desk, and following the step-by-step directions on the video, bent them into the proper shapes. Kneeling in front of the file cabinet, I inserted the paper clips as instructed into the lock's keyhole. After a minute or two of trial and error, the lock popped open.

I first slid out the bottom file drawer, groaning when I discovered the contents—a large metal lock box. I removed the box and placed it on the desk. After settling onto the desk chair, I grabbed the paper clips and hoped beginner's luck held for my second attempt at lock picking.

The lock box proved more difficult than the file cabinet, taking me fifteen minutes of fiddling with the paper clips before maneuvering them correctly into place to spring the lock. I raised the lid and gasped.

I'd come in contact with some badass guns over the last year, but the one nestled inside the box out-badassed all of them by a mile—even if I had no idea what it was. This gun made Zack's Mr. Sauer look like a toy. Alongside the gun sat a scope of some sort and what I believed might be a silencer since one end contained screw threads. A box of ammunition—labeled as hollow-point bullets—an envelope, and a large black velvet pouch with a drawstring rounded out the box's contents.

Not knowing whether or not the gun was loaded, I slid the envelope out from under it, taking care not to touch the gun.

Inside the envelope I found five passports, all with Lawrence's picture but issued in different names. Alvin Esposito. Claude LeBlanc. Donald Sarkasian. Franklin Quinn. Wilson Schmidt— Spanish, French, Armenian, Irish, German—Lawrence had covered a large segment of white male ethnicity. Was one of these names the real Lawrence Tuttnauer, or were they all aliases? I grabbed my cell phone and snapped photos of each passport. Then I returned the passports to the envelope and gingerly slid the envelope back under the gun.

Just when I thought nothing could shock me further, I opened the velvet pouch and blinked, not believing what twinkled back at me—four or five-dozen very large, exceedingly brilliant diamonds. I poured several into the palm of my hand, estimating each at three carats or larger. To my untrained eye, the diamonds appeared pretty darned flawless. I weighed the pouch in my hand, wondering how many millions of dollars I held. A couple of these babies would wipe out my Karl-induced debt, restore my bank accounts, and set my kids and me up for life.

For a nanosecond I wondered if Lawrence would miss a few diamonds among his cache. Then the moment fled, and I was left alone with my conscience. I poured the diamonds back into the pouch and placed the pouch inside the lock box.

Only then did I realize the flaw in my plan. I didn't have the key to relock the box. I grabbed my phone and searched for an answer on the Internet. Apparently, no one cared about alternate ways to relock a lock because I didn't find a single site that offered any help. I'd just have to hope Lawrence wouldn't notice the box was already unlocked the next time he went to open it.

Once I returned the lock box to the bottom drawer of the file cabinet, I pulled open the top drawer, which held thirty-five to forty file folders, each labeled with a long series of letters and numbers. I pulled out the first file and opened it to find a series of statements for a bank located in the Cayman Islands. The account belonged to Continental Machine Works, Inc. I snapped a photo of the top statement and returned the folder to the file.

The next folder I withdrew contained statements from another bank, this one located in Bermuda, and for another company, American Industries, Inc. I snapped a photo of that account's most recent statement. I quickly realized that each file contained bank statements from different banks in various countries and all under different company names.

As I stared at the folders lined up in the file, the truth stared back at me. Lawrence had never owned a commercial laundry; Lawrence laundered money for the mob.

My hands shook as I closed the open folder and slipped it back into the file drawer. I'd had enough run-ins with the Mafia to last me a lifetime. All I wanted to do was hightail it out of the condo and forget what I'd discovered. But how could I when I'd just learned my mother had married into the mob?

At that moment, though, I faced a more pressing dilemma as I heard the front door of the condo open. The alarm began to beep, and Mama called out, "Anastasia? Are you here, dear?"

SIXTEEN

What the hell were they doing home?

I couldn't let Lawrence catch me red-handed at his desk. I quickly closed the file drawer, realizing I had about fifteen seconds to come up with a plausible explanation as to why I was in the room. Luckily the file cabinet lock was the kind that locked by depressing the mechanism flush with the cabinet.

As soon as I'd clicked the lock into place, I stepped away from the desk and tossed my phone under the sofa. Then I flipped one of the cushions and dropped to my knees just as Mama and Lawrence entered the den.

"What in the world—?" asked Mama.

"What the hell's going on here?" asked Lawrence.

I stood, placed my hands on my lower back and stretched. "I can't find my phone. I thought maybe I dropped it here last night."

Mama's brows knit together. "But I spoke on the phone with you this morning, dear."

"I called you from my office phone. Anyway, I've searched all over—home, office. I even stopped at the diner we went to last night. This is the only other place I could think to look."

Lawrence whipped out his cell phone. "What's the number?"

I rattled off my cell number. A moment later the air filled with the sounds of an orchestral version of "I Am Woman," the music I'd chosen as my new ring-tone. Lawrence bent down and fished the phone out from under the sofa and handed it to me.

I shook my head and faked an exaggerated sigh of relief as I slipped the phone into my purse while I avoided looking directly at him. "What a relief! This phone isn't even a week old, and it cost me a fortune."

The phone actually hadn't cost me a penny, thanks to Zack's generosity, but Lawrence would never know that. I added an ironic chuckle. "Always the last place you look, right?"

Then I turned to Mama. "What are you doing home? I thought you were planning to spend the night out on Long Island."

"Some maniac ran a stop sign and plowed into us," she said.

My jaw dropped, and my stomach plummeted as I swept my gaze up and down Mama for signs of injury. No casts. No bruises. No swelling. No bandages. "Were you hurt?"

Lawrence answered for her. "We're both more shaken up than anything."

Mama placed her hands, one on top of the other, over her neckline and shuddered. "I swear my life flashed before me. I really and truly thought we would die."

"But you're both okay? Did you hit your heads?" I stood nose-to-nose with Mama, checking for dilated pupils.

"We're both fine," he said. "The hospital ran scans before they allowed us to leave."

"You were able to drive home?"

He nodded. "Luckily, the jerk only clipped the rear end of our car."

"Only?" Mama's voice climbed two octaves. "You make it sound like he just tapped our bumper." She turned to me. "The impact spun us around, and pushed us onto a sidewalk crowded with pedestrians. Somehow Lawrence managed to keep us from hitting a traffic light pole and several people walking down the street at the time."

She removed one hand from her neck, placed it on his forearm, and graced him with a worshipful smiled. "He not only saved our lives but the lives of all those other people."

I turned to Lawrence. "Thank you. I don't know what I'd do if anything happened to Mama."

He nodded.

"I'm going to soak in a hot tub," said Mama. "I may not have any injuries, but I feel like I was run over by a freight train."

"That's a good idea." I wrapped my arms around her and gave her a gentle hug. "I'm glad nothing worse happened. I'll call you tomorrow."

I grabbed my purse, waved goodbye to Lawrence, and left the condo. I was about to step into my car when someone grabbed my arm and spun me around.

"Want to tell me what you were really doing in the den?" asked Lawrence. He held out his hand to show me the two bent paperclips I'd forgotten on his desk.

Lying is definitely not my forte; I have a hard time looking someone in the eye and keeping a straight face. However, a little voice at the back of my brain told me my life might depend on whether or not I could pull off an Oscar-worthy performance at that moment.

I knit my brows together and stared at the misshapen bits of metal in Lawrence's hand, poking them with my index finger. "What in the world are those?" I asked.

"You tell me."

I raised my head, looked him straight in the eyes, and shrugged. "I have no idea." I ducked into my Jetta, locked the door, and started the engine, but before I drove away, I rolled down the window. "Have you heard the news?" I asked.

"What news?"

"Stevie "Jelly Bean" Benini is dead."

His face showed no emotion. "How?"

"He was found slumped over his steering wheel. No obvious signs of foul play, but an autopsy is scheduled to determine cause of death."

"I see."

"You don't look surprised."

"The man had a heart condition and smoked three packs a day. I told him nicotine would kill him sooner than any of his former associates."

I wondered, considering I'd once heard there were methods of murder that simulated the appearance of a fatal heart attack or actually caused one. But Lawrence couldn't have killed 'Jelly Bean,' not if he and Mama were on Long Island when 'Jelly Bean' died in Weehauken, New Jersey.

As I drove away from the condo, I hazarded a glance in the rearview mirror. Lawrence stood in the parking space I'd vacated, hands on hips, a scowl on his face, watching me drive away. An involuntary shudder coursed through my body.

~*~

My phone rang as I turned off the road leading from the condo and onto South Avenue. "Where are you?" asked Zack.

"Five minutes away."

"Where you stuck in traffic most of this time?"

"No, I ran into a slight problem."

"Define *slight problem*."

"I'll explain when I get home."

"Am I going to like the explanation?"

Doubtful but I didn't tell him that. An image of Zack as an angry cartoon character danced before my eyes. Red-faced with steam shooting out the top of his head, the animated Zack stamped his feet and pounded his fists in the air. "We'll talk when I get home." I hung up before he had a chance to say more.

The moment I pulled into the driveway, Zack ran out the kitchen door and stood beside the Jetta, waiting for me to cut the engine and step out of the car. He didn't even let me enter the house before he began peppering me with questions.

I placed a hand over his mouth. "I promise I'll tell you everything. Later. After dinner." That should give me enough time to compose myself and figure out what to say to him.

Of course, I'd tell Zack everything. How could I not? I just needed to do so in a manner that kept him from throttling me or locking me up and tossing away the key. Or maybe he'd throttle me first, then lock me up and toss away the key. No matter how I couched my condo escapade, Zack would shortly morph into one very unhappy guy.

Dinner consisted of Italian subs and chips, easy to eat in-between bouncing up to answer the door and hand out candy. We all took turns except for Lucille who, around every mouthful, offered a nonstop litany of anti-Halloween sentiment—the only opinion the two of us have ever shared.

As dinner progressed, the time between doorbell rings grew longer as the nonstop hordes of kids thinned to a now-and-then trickle. We were nearly finished with dinner when the bell rang once more. This time Zack hopped up to answer. He returned a moment later with Lawrence in tow.

My heart hammered a rapid staccato inside my chest, and I nearly lost my dinner.

Lawrence spoke directly to me, his face a slab of stone, showing no hint of emotion. No fear. No anger. "I'd like to speak with you, Anastasia." He then nodded toward Zack. "You, too." He swept a quick glance toward Alex, Nick, and Lucille. "In private if you don't mind."

I pushed myself away from the table. "Why don't we go into the den?"

I don't know how I made it from the dining room to the den without my legs buckling under me. Once in the room, Lawrence indicated that Zack and I should take seats on the couch. He began to pace back and forth in front of us. "There's something I need to tell you, but it can't go beyond this room. Do I have your word?"

"Does it have anything to do with Mama?" I asked.

He shook his head. "Nothing other than I want to spare her any needless worry."

Zack and I both agreed.

Lawrence took a deep breath. "The recent events over the weekend and earlier this evening lead me to believe the two of you suspect me of some nefarious activities."

"What happened this evening?" asked Zack. "And aren't you supposed to be on Long Island?"

Lawrence turned to me. "You haven't told him?"

"Told me what?" asked Zack.

"I haven't had a chance. I was waiting until after dinner."

Lawrence nodded. "No need to go into that now, then.

Everything will become clear shortly."

He resumed his pacing. "As I suspect Anastasia has already discovered, Lawrence Tuttnauer is not my real name."

"Who are you?" asked Zack.

"I'd rather not say, but you'll understand why if you allow me to continue."

Zack indicated with a nod for Lawrence to proceed.

"Cynthia came by her drug addiction naturally. Doctors will tell you addiction is often hereditary. Cynthia's mother died of a heroin overdose. We were living in Carson City, Nevada. Cynthia was a teenager at the time."

"What did you do?" I asked.

Lawrence pulled his lips into a tight, thin line. His eyes grew demonic. "I found her dealer and dealt with him."

From the look on his face I knew there was no need to pose my next words in the form of a question. "You killed him."

"Not until I'd forced enough information from him to use as a bargaining chip with the police. I gave them everything they needed to take down the largest heroin operation in Nevada in exchange for my freedom."

"Are you in WitSec?" asked Zack.

"They offered, but I had other resources that provided me better protection."

"Benini?"

Lawrence nodded. "There are many benefits to having a cousin high up the ranks in the mob. For the right price you can buy anything from a new identity to a new face for yourself and your daughter, along with arranging a certain drug kingpin never lives long enough to serve his time and walk out of prison."

He stopped pacing and stood in front of me. "I don't know what you did or didn't discover this evening," he said, "but I've made certain I have the means to leave quickly and undetected should the circumstances ever arise."

"I don't understand. You just admitted to killing Cynthia's dealer and having the drug kingpin killed in prison."

"I did. But the kingpin had many associates, some of whom escaped arrest and have since taken over his operation. I can't grow complacent. I've never had to execute my plan, but I have the peace of mind of knowing one exists should the situation arise."

"And Mama?"

"I'd make sure she was taken care of."

I hope he meant that in a good way. "And what about 'Jelly Bean' Benini?"

"Stevie was more than family; he was a true friend. It's a damn shame he didn't take better care of himself."

"He wasn't also your bookie?"

Lawrence sighed. "I suppose full disclosure is in order. Yes, Stevie was also my bookie. He's still in the mob, but as I suspect you discovered, I have more than enough money to frequent the casinos or place an occasional sports bet. I'm not in debt to the mob or anyone." He paused for a moment and smiled. "And I want to thank you for your honesty, Anastasia. A lesser person, especially one in your financial circumstances, wouldn't have thought twice, given the temptation."

Which meant Lawrence knew exactly how many diamonds were in that black velvet pouch. Not bowing to that temptation may have saved me from being fitted with a pair of cement shoes.

"What's that supposed to mean?" asked Zack.

I squeezed his hand and said, "I'll tell you later."

Lawrence left shortly after making his confession. As soon as Zack closed the front door behind him, he laced his fingers through mine and quickly marched me to the bedroom. However,

I knew romance was the furthest thing from his mind at the moment. He closed the bedroom door and spun me around to face him. "What happened at the condo this evening?"

I retrieved my purse from where I'd tossed it on the bed earlier and dug out my phone. After accessing the photos, I held up the phone to him and swiped across the passport photos. "This is part of Lawrence's insurance policy."

"How did you get these?"

I explained my lock-picking escapade. "The lock box also contained a few million dollars worth of diamonds—the temptation Lawrence mentioned—and a gun that makes yours look like a water pistol."

"How did Lawrence find out that you'd broken into the lock box?"

I frowned. "When the urge to snoop overtook me, I didn't realize that spying takes a certain amount of pre-planning. I made a couple of novice mistakes." I explained how I hadn't been able to lock the box afterwards and had forgotten that I left the paper clips I'd formed into picking tools on the desk.

Zack combed his fingers through his hair and huffed out a breath of frustration. "Look, I don't know exactly what Lawrence is mixed up in, if anything, but I can't help thinking this visit was more than a way of explaining what you discovered."

"Meaning?"

"Meaning it may also have been a warning to you to stop snooping around his life."

"Because he has connections and has ways of getting things done?"

"Exactly."

"Do you believe his story about Nevada?"

"It makes sense, but there are easy enough ways to check it

out."

"I discovered something else. Lawrence may not be aware that I saw these since I was able to lock the file cabinet." I scrolled to the bank statements. "Benini wasn't the only family member in the mob. These are but a few of the dozens of bank accounts, all from different banks and in the names of different companies. I didn't have time to photograph all of them."

Zack stared at the last image on the phone and whistled under his breath. "I think you discovered what Lawrence is mixed up in. He's laundering money for the mob."

"That was my guess. Possibly in exchange for those new identities he secured for himself and Cynthia."

"That's certainly a logical assumption."

"I figured as much. After all, how often does the mob do a favor for someone without expecting something in return?"

Zack didn't have to say anything. We both knew the answer to that question was *never*.

SEVENTEEN

Mr. Sandman decided to skip my house that night. I lay awake for hours, sick with worry over my mother. Part of me wanted to tell her both what I'd learned and what I suspected about her new husband, but when I played out every possible conversation in my head, each scenario concluded in ways I'd rather not imagine. Unfortunately those scenarios still succeeded in etching themselves into my brain.

Mama was definitely better off living in blissful ignorance. Lawrence had fooled quite a few people for a very long time. Better that Mama never learned she could now add Mafia Princess as another royal connection on her family tree.

Zack slept peacefully beside me. Figuring at least one of us should be able to get some shuteye, I fought the urge to toss and turn to avoid waking him. I forced my body to remain perfectly still and tried first to count sheep, then meditate myself to sleep. Neither worked. My brain refused to power down.

Still wide-awake at three in the morning, I slipped out of bed and silently made my way into the kitchen. After warming a cup of milk, I curled up on the couch in the den. As I sipped the warm milk, I surfed the TV for some mindless program that might bore me enough to put me to sleep.

Instead, I flipped from a cat food commercial to *The Godfather* just as Moe Greene took a bullet to his eye. I stared at the television as my sleep-deprived brain began playing tricks on me, suddenly morphing Moe Greene on a massage table in Las Vegas to Betty Bentworth sitting on her couch in Westfield. Both killed in much the same way and neither saw it coming.

"Can't sleep?"

I nearly jumped out of my skin as the remote flew from my hand and the mug toppled onto my lap. My bathrobe took on the role of sponge, quickly sucking up the remaining milk. Luckily, I'd drained all but an ounce or two before Zack nearly gave me a heart attack.

Once my heart started pumping again, I slipped out of the wet robe and scowled at him. "Jeez! You scared the crap out of me."

He stepped into the den, stooped to pick up the remote, and glanced at the TV before clicking it off. "Me? You're the one watching Michael Corleone eliminate his competition." He pulled an afghan off the back of the sofa and wrapped it around me.

"I was searching for something mind-numbing to help me sleep."

"Multiple Mafia executions? Poor choice."

"I'll say." But after making the analogy between Moe Greene's and Betty Bentworth's murders, something now niggled at the edges of my brain. I frowned as I searched for the puzzle pieces just beyond my grasp.

Then it hit me. "This can't be coincidence."

"What?"

"All the murders."

"*The Godfather* murders?"

I shook my head. "No, the ones over the last week. There *is* a connection that links them. Pablo. Betty. Carmen." My synapses were firing so fast and furiously in my head, I felt like my brain could supply power to half of New Jersey.

Zack lowered himself onto the coffee table in front of the sofa. Our knees touching, he reached for my hands and clasped them in his. A concerned look creased his brow. "Want to back up and clue me in as to what's spinning around in that brain of yours?"

"While you were off doing your spy thing in Greece—"

"You mean my photojournalism assignment in Amphipolis?"

I waved away the difference. "Whatever." We'd have to agree to disagree on that until Zack chose to come clean with me. "Anyway, Mama invited Ira and his kids here for dinner. During the meal, Ira received a phone call from one of the detectives investigating Cynthia's death. Afterwards he blurted out in front of his kids the manner in which Pablo was killed, and Isaac said it was just like a scene from *Breaking Bad*."

"Ira let his kids watch *Breaking Bad*?" Zack shook his head. "Talk about poor parenting skills."

"I know, but forget about Ira for now. Pablo was strangled with a bicycle lock, certainly not a common murder weapon. Isaac said someone on *Breaking Bad* was killed the same way. And when we were at Carmen's house, Lupe said her mother was stabbed while taking a shower—"

"Like the scene in *Psycho*."

"Exactly. And Betty's murder—"

"Is similar to the killing of Moe Greene in *The Godfather*. I have to agree with you, this seems awfully coincidental, but it could be just that, nothing more than a weird coincidence."

"Maybe." I wasn't convinced. "At first I thought Spader was crazy when he kept asking me if I'd pissed anyone off recently, but maybe he's not as off-base as I thought. I know it doesn't make any sense, but it appears I'm the connection that ties all of these murders together."

"But you never met Pablo. How would his death have anything to do with Betty and Carmen? They occurred clear across the state."

I shook my head. "Not just Pablo's death. Maybe Cynthia's death as well."

"How do you figure that?"

"Humor me. Can you think of any movie or TV episode where a murder is made to appear like a drug overdose?"

Zack pondered for a moment. "I can think of a couple of older movies—*Michael Clayton* and *The Juror*. No recent ones come to mind—at least none I've seen—but there are probably some."

"I know this sounds crazy, but what if Spader is wrong about Carmen and Betty being murdered by two separate killers? What if it was the same person using different methods to throw off the police?"

"That's certainly possible, but how do the murders of Carmen and Betty have anything to do with Cynthia and Pablo? Other than you knowing three of the four victims, what could possibly tie them together?"

I fought without success to stifle a yawn. "I don't know, but maybe Detective Spader needs to have a conversation with the homicide detectives investigating Cynthia's and Pablo's deaths in Hunterdon and Camden Counties."

Zack pulled me to my feet. "Call him tomorrow to discuss your theory. For now I'm taking you back to bed."

~*~

The next morning, after a quick stop in the break room to grab a cup of coffee and an oatmeal apple muffin, I placed a call to Detective Spader. "What can I do for you, Mrs. Pollack?" he asked after coming on the line.

"I need to speak with you about Carmen's and Betty's murders."

He expelled a sigh of annoyance. "You know I'm not at liberty to discuss ongoing cases with you."

"Even if it might lead to an arrest?"

That caught his attention. "Is there something you haven't shared with me? I'm sure I don't have to remind you that withholding evidence is a criminal offense."

"I haven't withheld anything from you, Detective; I just figured this out last night."

"Figured what out?"

"I think you're dealing with one killer."

"How did—" He stopped himself short. Then he said, "Not possible. The M.O.'s are completely different. You're wasting my time."

"We really need to talk, Detective. If I'm right, the killer is responsible for two more murders."

"What murders?"

"One in Hunterdon County about three weeks ago and another in Camden County two weeks later."

He let loose a not so mild expletive. "Where are you, Mrs. Pollack?"

"At my office."

"Give me the address. I'm on my way."

For someone who moments earlier complained I was wasting his time, Spader had certainly executed a lightning speed about-face. I mulled that bit of information over as I took another bite of muffin.

"Skip breakfast again?" asked Cloris, popping into my cubicle.

I nodded, my mouth full of muffin, then washed it down with a swig of coffee before speaking. "I couldn't get out of bed this morning. It was either breakfast or arriving at work on time. I figured I could count on you to provide me with morning sustenance."

"Rough night?"

"I'm operating on less than three hours sleep." I then proceeded to tell her everything that had transpired since I left work yesterday. I finished by adding, "Spader's on his way over here now."

Cloris stared wide-eyed at me, shaking her head. "Your life is more far-fetched than some zany mystery novel. Mafia, murders, and money laundering—not to mention a swatting incident— same-old/same-old in the everyday life of *American Woman's* intrepid crafts editor sleuth. Maybe I should start taking notes. I could be the next Janet Evanovich."

"Don't forget the communist mother-in-law and the Shakespeare-quoting parrot."

Cloris rolled her eyes. "Heaven forbid! How could I possibly forget Lucille and Ralph?"

I laughed in spite of myself. "If it weren't my own life, I wouldn't believe it, either."

"I'm serious about the book. If you don't want to write one, I will."

I waved Cloris away. "Have at it. I don't have time for breakfast most days. When would I find time to write a book?"

~*~

Forty-five minutes later the receptionist called to say Detective Spader had arrived. I met him in the lobby and led him upstairs to the conference room where we could talk without interruption.

He wedged himself into one of the butternut faux-leather upholstered chairs lining our well-worn walnut conference table. Even though our building is new, except for the custom designed fourth floor offices of the bigwigs, the Trimedia bean counters had saved a bundle by moving all our crappy old furniture from lower Manhattan to our new digs in the middle of a Morris County cornfield.

"So why am I here, Mrs. Pollack? What's this about other murders?"

Where to begin? I inhaled deeply, expelling the air slowly while I paced back and forth to gather my thoughts. "Bear with me, Detective. This is going to take some explaining." I then began to tell him about Cynthia's body being found in the canal and Pablo turning up dead in Camden.

He looked up from his notepad and asked, "What's your connection to these murders?"

"Cynthia was married to my husband's half-brother Ira. Her father married my mother. You've seen them. They arrived at my house the night I discovered Betty's body."

He nodded. "And Pablo?"

"Ira's pool boy. He and Cynthia were having an affair. They ran off together a couple of weeks before Cynthia's body was pulled out of the canal."

After jotting another note, Spader said, "The Hunterdon County police are most likely looking at Cynthia's husband as their prime suspect."

I raised an eyebrow. Did Spader already know about Cynthia's death? And if so, why? Lambertville was way out of his jurisdiction. "What makes you say that?"

"He's the most logical suspect."

"But Ira had nothing to do with Cynthia's death."

Now it was Spader turn to raise an eyebrow. "You know this for a fact?"

Point taken. I had no proof Ira wasn't responsible for Cynthia's death—just my gut telling me Ira was no killer.

"What do these murders have to do with my cases, Mrs. Pollack?"

"The medical examiner ruled Cynthia's death an overdose. Lawrence claimed she had an ongoing drug problem, but Ira knew nothing about that and never saw any signs of drug use."

"What about you?"

"I only met Cynthia once. She acted perfectly normal." For a stuck-up gold-digger looking down her nose at her husband's poor relations, I added to myself. "I didn't notice any telltale specks of white powder under her nose or any other visible signs of drug use."

"If her death was ruled a drug overdose, why do you suspect foul play?"

"I don't believe the accuracy of the medical examiner's report."

This time Spader raised both eyebrows. I quickly explained my theory about the manner in which all the victims had been killed. "I think it's one killer using methods from various movies and TV shows so the police won't connect the murders."

Now Spader went from raised eyebrows to rolling his eyes. "You dragged me all the way out here for this flimsy crock of circumstantial evidence? Stay away from the television, Mrs. Pollack." He pushed his chair back and stood to leave.

I stopped dead in my tracks and leaned against the conference door to block his exit. "Wait! There's more."

Spader placed his hands on the table and leaned toward me. "You have one minute. And for cripe's sake, sit down. You're making me dizzy with all that pacing." He pointed to the chair at a right angle to his.

I dropped into the seat. He remained standing, his arms folded across his chest, as I continued. "The reason I think all the murders are tied together is because of Lawrence."

"Lawrence?" He grabbed his pad and referred to his notes, scowling as he flipped several pages. "Who's Lawrence?"

"My mother's new husband. Lawrence Tuttnauer."

Spader raised his head. "Your mother married Lawrence Tuttnauer?"

I nodded. "You know him?"

"I'm asking the questions here, Mrs. Pollack." He lowered himself back into the chair.

"And I've always been not only forthright and honest with you, Detective, but exceedingly helpful. I should think by now you know you can trust me."

He eyed me for a moment before grunting something that might or might not have been his way of offering an apology. "You're right. Let's just say I've heard the name mentioned in the past." He waved his hand in the air. "Go on."

"Has his name come up in an organized crime investigation? Because I have reason to believe he's laundering money for the Genovese mob."

Spader's brow wrinkled as his eyes narrowed. He took his seat, leaned back, and crossed his arms over his chest. "Go on."

I told him what Lawrence had explained to Zack and me about the events in Carson City and how he'd turned down the government's offer of Witness Protection. "Lawrence's cousin is that mobster who died yesterday—"Jelly Bean" Benini. He arranged for new identities for Lawrence and his daughter, I'm guessing in exchange for laundering mob money. Lawrence didn't say, but the mob just doesn't do favors for people without expecting something in return."

"And how do you know that, Mrs. Pollack?"

I rolled my eyes. "Really, Detective? I live in New Jersey. How would I not know that?"

He grunted again. "So why would Lawrence Tuttnauer tell you all this?"

"He realized I'd discovered some questionable items he'd locked away—passports in various names, a cache of diamonds, a gun. He explained why he had them."

"Which was?"

"In case he ever had to make a quick getaway. I don't think he realized I had also discovered evidence of the money laundering."

Pencil poised over his notepad, Spader made direct eye contact with me and asked, "Exactly how did you discover all this evidence?"

I squirmed in my seat. "I was snooping through his desk."

Spader slammed his notebook onto the conference table. "You suspect your mother's husband is connected to organized crime, and you—" He sputtered, unable to continue his train of thought. Then he finally said, "Are you out of your freaking mind, Mrs. Pollack, or just incredibly stupid?"

"Neither. And I didn't know he was in the mob when I started looking through his desk. I thought he had a gambling problem and owed Benini money. I was concerned for my mother's wellbeing."

Spader lowered his head and ran both hands through what remained of his hair. Was it my imagination, or was he counting to ten under his breath? "Okay. I suppose that's understandable."

"What are you going to do?"

He gathered his notepad and pencil, pushed away from the

table, and stood. "My job."

"What should I do?"

"Keep your mouth shut and your nose out of everything that doesn't concern you."

"This concerns me."

Spader glared at me. "You know what I mean. No more snooping. Leave the investigating to the professionals. I don't want you getting hurt. Understood?"

I nodded. "Don't take too long."

He stormed out of the conference room, slamming the door behind him.

EIGHTEEN

I have to admit I was surprised to find Mama and Lawrence at my house when I returned from work later that evening. I would have thought Lawrence might fear I'd blab to Mama what I knew about him and therefore, want to keep the two of us as far apart as possible. Apparently, his Dinner Mooching gene outweighed his concerns about my big mouth. Either that or he realized I'd never say anything that might cause Mama distress. Whatever the reason, once again I had two extra mouths to feed at Casa Pollack that night.

I found Mama and Lawrence curled up on the sofa, watching the six o'clock news on the den television. I took a deep breath and exhaled my annoyance. "Mama, I really wish you'd give me some notice when you plan to join us for dinner. I don't know that I have enough meatloaf to feed everyone."

At that moment my phone chimed an incoming text. I ignored it as Mama waved away my concern. "We'll make do, dear. You can always open a few cans of soup as a first course and make a larger salad."

"Wouldn't you prefer the peace and quiet of dinner at your condo where you won't get into any arguments with Lucille? You know how she irritates you."

Lawrence pulled his attention away from a traffic report about a pile-up on the George Washington Bridge. "That would mean I'd have to eat your mother's cooking."

Mama jabbed him in the ribs. "Very funny! As I often remind you, dear, you didn't marry me for my culinary skills."

"Good thing. I'd starve."

"My talents lie elsewhere," said Mama.

Lawrence lifted her hand off her lap and kissed her palm. "And those talents are a far better use of your time."

Mama batted her lashes while I placed my hands over my ears and loudly proclaimed, "TMI!"

My mother stopped her eyelash batting and turned to me. "Our being here has nothing to do with my cooking. I don't like the idea of you and the boys alone in the house while there's a killer on the loose."

"We're not alone. Zack is here, and I have a security system." Besides, what sort of protection could two oversexed senior citizens provide should a killer come calling?

Although, given what I now knew about Lawrence, perhaps having him around wasn't such a bad idea, especially if he came armed. I wondered if he owned more than the one gun I found locked away in his desk.

"Where are the boys?" I asked, changing the subject as I unbuttoned my coat and removed the scarf wrapped around my neck. Alex and Nick were nowhere in sight. For that matter, neither was Zack.

"I think they're in Zack's apartment," said Mama. "When do

you plan on serving dinner, dear? We're famished."

"I'll have the maître d' call you when your table is ready."

"Really, Anastasia, sarcasm is not becoming."

"Neither are uninvited dinner guests," I mumbled under my breath as I exited the den.

"What's that, dear? You know I can't hear you when you mumble."

Which is why I mumbled. "Nothing, Mama. Just talking to myself," I called back.

My phone chimed again as I made my way to the kitchen. I fished it out of my purse and glanced at the display to find a message from Zack: *Meet me in apt.*

I deposited my purse on the kitchen table, then grabbed the meatloaf out of the refrigerator and tossed it into the oven to heat up. After wrapping my scarf back around my neck, I headed out the back door.

Zack was waiting for me at the top of the staircase and ushered me inside. I looked around as I slipped out of my coat. "I thought the boys were with you."

"I wanted them out of the house."

"What do you mean? Where are they?"

"I treated them to dinner out. Told them to head over to the library afterwards to do their homework and not come home until we called them."

"Why? What's going on?"

"Sit down."

His serious tone caused all my nerve endings to stand at attention. I made my way over to the sofa while he grabbed a bottle of chardonnay from the refrigerator, uncorked it, and brought it, along with two wine glasses, to where I now sat nervously on the edge of one of the sofa cushions.

"I made a few phone calls today," he said, filling the glasses and handing me one before taking a seat beside me.

"To whom?"

"People I know in Washington."

"Alphabet people?"

He frowned. "I know people who know people. I called in a few favors."

I took a sip of wine. "And?"

"No one could confirm the story Lawrence told us about what happened in Carson City."

"He lied to us?"

"About everything. There's nothing in any law enforcement database about a man killing a drug dealer after his wife overdosed and nothing about anyone striking a deal to get out of a murder conviction for testifying against a major Nevada drug kingpin who subsequently was murdered in prison."

"How far back did they look? Lawrence said the events occurred when Cynthia was a teenager."

"And I'm telling you they never happened. Lawrence pulled the entire story out of his butt."

I could think of only one reason why Lawrence would make up such a fantastical story—to cover up something far worse. "What should we do? I'm worried about Mama. Who knows what Lawrence has done or what he's capable of doing."

"I've already notified Detective Spader. Apparently, he has his own suspicions about Lawrence. Once you told him what you'd discovered, he contacted the county Organized Crime Task Force. They're going to execute a search of the condo."

"When?"

Zack shrugged. "Depends. They have to wait until a judge signs off on the warrant."

"Which means they could be searching the condo right now?"

"Possibly."

"Spader told you all this?"

"Yes."

Spader never told me anything, no matter how helpful I've been to him. All I ever got was the standard line about not being able to divulge any information regarding an ongoing investigation. Was this a case of bro-bonding out of professional courtesy or gender discrimination on the part of a male chauvinist cop?

I itched to call Zack out on this, but now was not the time. Instead I asked, "So Lawrence has no idea about any of this?"

"Of course not."

"Does Spader know Lawrence is here now?"

"I called him as soon as I got the boys out of the house. We have to pretend everything is completely normal here this evening."

I nodded even though I found myself two breaths away from a panic attack. I didn't do deceit convincingly. "But how will the police get into the condo without setting off the alarm? Won't the alarm company notify Lawrence of a breach?"

"You need to trust that the police know what they're doing. It's quite possible they may delay executing the warrant until after Lawrence and your mother return home this evening."

How does he know all this? My list of reasons why Zack was really a spy continued to grow, but I had a bigger worry at the moment. "Whether the police wait or not, they're going to seize all those files I discovered—along with the gun, the diamonds, and whatever else they find. And it's not going to take a rocket scientist to figure out I had something to do with it."

Zack reached for my free hand and squeezed it. "He's going to be arrested tonight."

That didn't keep me from quaking in my shoes—shoes that might soon become encased in cement, given Lawrence's connections. "Prison bars are no guarantee he won't seek revenge."

"I spoke to Spader about that. He assured me that won't be the case."

"Why not? Lawrence is going to know someone ratted him out, and I'm the obvious rat."

"Unless they have another rat feeding them information."

"Who?"

Zack shrugged. "That's on a need-to-know basis."

"Need-to-know basis?" I jumped to my feet; my voice escalated three octaves. "Shouldn't I of all people need to know? Given Lawrence knows I rifled through his belongings, he'll target me as top rat on his list."

Before Zack could answer we heard someone climbing the stairs to the apartment. A moment later the door opened, and Mama entered. "What's all the shouting about?"

Zack frowned at her. "Perhaps you could knock next time, Flora?"

She ignored him and instead turned her attention to me. Waving at the wine glasses and the half-empty bottle of chardonnay sitting on the coffee table, she said, "Since the two of you don't seem to be enjoying a very happy Happy Hour, do you think we could get on with dinner? Some of us are hungry— including the belligerent Bolshevik who's downstairs hurling all sorts of insults your way. She thinks you're up here enjoying an early evening delight."

If only...

I grabbed the half-empty wine bottle and handed it to her.

"Dinner isn't ready yet. Why don't you and Lawrence enjoy a glass of wine in the meantime? Offer one to Lucille, too."

Mama studied the contents of the bottle. "There's hardly enough here for two glasses, let alone three."

Zack grabbed a bottle of pinot noir from his wine rack, passed it to her, and swung open the door. "Enjoy, Flora."

After glancing at the label, Mama graced him with one of her Blanche Dubois smiles. "Isn't that sweet of you, Zachary dear." Then she frowned and added, "Although it's a shame to waste such good wine on that commie pinko."

"Mama—"

"Well, it's true." She executed a graceful pirouette and flounced down the stairs.

As soon as Zack closed the door behind her, I smacked my hand against my forehead and groaned. "You know what's the worst part of all this?"

"What?"

"If Lawrence is arrested and goes to prison, she won't be able to afford to stay in that condo. She'll wind up back here permanently."

"Not permanently. Only until she finds her next husband."

"How comforting. I'll tell you one thing, though. If she wants to get married again, I'm hiring a detective to vet the next guy before she sashays down the aisle again. I don't care how much it costs."

Although, I was beginning to regret not having helped myself to at least one of those diamonds, which I'm sure the government would confiscate. I also wondered what would happen to all that money socked away in those offshore bank accounts.

I gulped down the remainder of wine in my glass, took a deep breath, and said, "Let's get this dinner over with."

Zack and I headed downstairs and into the house. With Ralph observing from his favorite spot atop the refrigerator, I tossed a batch of sweet potato fries into the toaster oven, then started chopping up a salad. After feeding Ralph a piece of carrot, Zack grabbed plates and silverware to set the dining room table.

Right on cue, the moment Zack began to set the table, Lucille waddled precariously into the dining room. I watched from the kitchen as she lugged a squirming Mephisto under one arm while maneuvering her cane with her other hand. As she collapsed onto her chair, the poor dog wriggled out of her grasp and scampered off to join me in the kitchen.

When the meatloaf and rice were ready, I called Mama and Lawrence to the table. Ralph followed me in from the kitchen and perched himself atop the breakfront. Mephisto remained camped out on the kitchen floor next to his water and food bowls.

"Where are the boys?" asked Mama, noticing only five place settings.

"They have dinner plans," I said.

She raised one of her perfectly waxed eyebrows. "On a school night?"

"It's a student government planning session," I lied, not looking directly at her or anyone else at the table.

I kept my head down and remained silent for most of the meal. Of course, Mama noticed. "That must have been some fight the two you had."

Ralph spread his wings and squawked. "*Now put your shields before your hearts, and fight with hearts more proof than shields. Coriolanus.* Act One, Scene Four."

"We weren't fighting," I said.

"Certainly sounded like a fight to me," said Mama.

Zack placed his hand under the table and squeezed my thigh.

"Anastasia is tired, Flora. She had a rough day at work and arrived home to find unexpected dinner company."

"We're hardly company," said Mama. "We're family."

I opened my mouth to say something but thought better of it. Why stoke the fire? All I wanted was dinner to end and my *company* to leave. The sooner the better. At least Mama hadn't invited Ira and his brood to join us this evening.

However, Lucille exercised no such discretion. "That doesn't give you the right to waltz in here whenever you want," she said.

"No one asked for your commie two cents," said Mama.

"I don't need your permission," said Lucille. "I live here."

Before Mama could respond, the doorbell rang. "Saved by the bell," I muttered, pushing back from the table.

Zack placed his hand on my shoulder. "Finish your dinner. I'll get it."

A moment later he returned with Detective Spader and two uniformed officers.

"Oh my!" said Mama. "Are we being sweated again?"

"Swatted," said Lawrence. He eyed me, his expression malevolent. "And I don't believe so. Isn't that right, Anastasia?"

"I have no idea—"

"Oh, I think you do." Lawrence yanked Mama out of her chair, whipped a gun from his waistband, and pointed it at her head.

NINETEEN

"Here's what's going to happen," said Lawrence in a calm voice completely incongruous with the situation. "My wife and I are going to walk out of here. Anyone tries to stop us and I splatter her brains all over the dining room."

"Lawrence!" Mama screamed as she tried to twist out of his grasp. "What are you doing? Are you crazy? You're hurting me. Let me go!"

He twisted her arm nearly to the breaking point and pressed the gun into her temple. "Keep your mouth shut, Flora."

The color drained from Mama's face. Her chin trembled; she began to hyperventilate. I feared she might pass out in his arms.

Lawrence waved the gun at the three policemen and Zack. "Down on the floor. All of you. Faces down. Hands behind your heads."

"Do as he says," said Spader, lowering himself to the carpet.

Once they were all prone, Lawrence pointed the gun at me. "Remove their weapons. Try anything stupid and your mother dies."

"You can't possibly think you're going to get away with this," I said as I stepped toward Spader. I pulled the service weapon from his shoulder holster, not an easy task given his bulk, his position on the floor, and the fact that he didn't seem inclined to make my task any easier by shifting his weight. However, under the circumstances, I could hardly blame him.

Lawrence chuckled. "Of course, I will. You think I haven't done this before?"

"Why don't you put the gun down and tell me all about it?"

"Why don't you shut up and do as you're told?"

For the briefest of seconds I thought about aiming Spader's gun at him, but I'd never fired a gun before, and I seriously doubted Lawrence was bluffing about killing Mama. My hand trembled as I held the gun out to him.

"Place it in the center of the table," he said.

I did as I was told and moved on to the first uniformed officer.

Now would be a fabulous time for Zack to prove me right about working for one of those alphabet agencies—especially if he happened to have Mr. Sauer hidden somewhere on him. Lawrence would never suspect Zack might be armed, and unlike me, I bet Zack had quite a bit of gun experience.

If ever I needed a James Bond sort of guy in my life, this was the time. I made quick eye contact with Zack, but unfortunately his expression gave no indication of what might be spinning around in his head.

Once I'd removed all three guns and placed them on the dining room table, Lawrence said, "Now get down on the floor with the others and place your hands behind your head. You, too," he said, pointing the gun at Lucille.

"Absolutely not."

Lawrence dragged Mama closer to Lucille and stuck the gun in my mother-in-law's face. "Now or you're the first to die. And you have no idea how much pleasure killing you would give me."

"Do as he says, Lucille. Please, before someone gets hurt."

She turned to glare at me. "This is all your fault, Anastasia." Then with a huge grunt she slowly leveraged herself up from the table. She grabbed her cane and hobbled a step toward an empty spot on the floor, but before Lawrence realized what she was doing, she pivoted, slipped her cane between his legs, and yanked with both hands, sending him and Mama sprawling to the floor.

Ralph flapped his wings and squawked wildly as the gun flew from Lawrence's hand, arcing into the air before landing inches from my head and discharging. The bullet ricocheted off my chandelier, raining glass shards, before hitting Lawrence in the foot.

Over the ringing in my ears I heard Lawrence let loose with a string of curses as he lunged for the gun. I beat him to it, sweeping my arm across the carpet to send the gun skidding under the base of the dining room table. Zack bounded off the floor and tackled Lawrence while Spader pushed himself to his feet and the two officers raced for their guns. A moment later three weapons were pointed at Lawrence's head.

Mephisto toddled into the dining room. After scoping out the situation, he planted himself alongside Lawrence's face, bared his teeth, and let loose a menacing growl.

I helped my mother off the floor, then turned to my soon-to-be-ex stepfather. "You may have done this before, but you won't be doing it again."

"I'll see you pay for this," he said as the uniformed officers yanked him up on his one good foot and cuffed him.

"She had nothing to do with this," said Spader.

"She had everything to do with it," said Lawrence. "I know a rat when I smell one."

Spader shook his head. "Think again. Salvatore Capperato, you're under arrest for orchestrating the murders of Cynthia Tuttnauer Pollack—AKA Cynthia Capperato—, Pablo Perez, Betty Bentworth, and Carmen Cordova. You have the right to remain silent—"

Mama spun around to face Spader. "Salvatore Capperato? There's no one here by that name. You're making a terrible mistake."

"I'm afraid you've been duped," said Spader.

"I know the man I married," said Mama, "and it's definitely not someone named Salvatore Capperato."

My jaw dropped as Spader ignored Mama and continued to inform Lawrence—Salvatore—of his rights. The man killed his own daughter? And Pablo, Betty, and Carmen? Obviously, my wild theory about one killer imitating TV and movie murders had proven correct. But why? What possible connection could the man we all knew as Lawrence Tuttnauer have to Betty Bentworth and Carmen Cordova?

"Lawrence," pleaded Mama, "tell them they're wrong. Please!"

He ignored her. For a brief moment a look of stunned surprise had overcome him. He quickly recovered and said, "You can't pin any of that on me. You have no proof."

"We have all the proof we need—a confession from "Jelly Bean" Benini, the man you hired to do your dirty work."

Relief swept over Lawrence, and he laughed. "You plan to put a dead man on the witness stand? Good luck with that."

Spader smiled. "Benini is very much alive. We staged his death after he sang like a canary when we offered him a deal."

I don't know who appeared more dumbfounded, Lawrence or

me. I glanced over at Zack. "Need-to-know," he mouthed.

I scowled at him. What I needed to know right now was how to get Zack, who apparently now had quite the intimate professional relationship with Detective Spader, to sing like a canary to me.

Spader called for two ambulances, one for Lawrence and one for Mama, insisting she get checked out at the hospital. If nothing else, Mama needed a strong sedative. I'd never seen her this confused and distraught. Zack and I followed the ambulance. "Details," I demanded as we pulled out of the driveway. "Now."

"I don't have many."

"But you knew Benini was alive?"

He nodded. "The forensics report came back on Carmen. They found a small trace of Benini's DNA on her and picked him up."

"And he fingered Lawrence/Salvatore?"

"For a laundry list of criminal activities. Between the indictments coming down from the county, the state, and the Feds, Salvatore Capperato—AKA Lawrence Tuttnauer and a dozen other alias—will spend the remainder of his life behind bars."

~*~

Mama's blood pressure concerned the doctors enough to keep her overnight for observation. I considered that a blessing.

Spader met us at the hospital after booking Salvatore at headquarters. He ushered us down the hall to an empty family lounge and indicated we should take seats at a small round table located in the center of the room. "How much have you told her?" he asked Zack.

The question made me bristle. "I'm right here, Detective. How about you start from the beginning and tell me everything yourself?"

Spader made eye contact with Zack. Zack nodded. "She deserves to know."

"Damn right, I deserve to know," I said, "considering I cracked this case wide open for you, Detective."

"Actually, Benini did that with his DNA match," he said.

"What about the bank statements, passports, and diamonds I found?"

"The state Organized Crime Task Force has you to thank for that," he conceded. "They'll be filing additional charges against Capperato. As will the Feds."

He stood and walked over to a coffee station in the corner of the room, popped in a pod, and waited for the cardboard cup to fill. "Anyone else?" he asked.

Both Zack and I declined. I was already too wired. A cup of coffee at this hour would keep me awake all night, not something I wanted after last night's insomnia.

Coffee in hand, Spader returned to the table. "I wasn't quite honest with you a minute ago, Mrs. Pollack. You do deserve some credit. I doubt Benini would have copped to the Hunterdon County murders if not for you mentioning them to me."

"Why did Capperato want Cynthia dead?" I asked.

"She became a liability. Perez was collateral damage. Capperato had no way of knowing what Cynthia may have told him. According to Benini, Capperato's daughter tried to blackmail him. He needed to shut her up."

"Blackmail him over what?"

"Part of the story he told you about Nevada had some grains of truth to it. His first wife did die but not from an overdose. He killed her. Cynthia somehow discovered the truth. That's probably why she started using drugs."

"He didn't testify against a drug kingpin?"

"There was no drug kingpin. Benini claims Capperato caught his wife cheating on him. He killed the guy, too. Not in Carson City, though. They lived in Houston. The bodies were never found. Capperato told everyone his wife ran off with her lover. No one suspected foul play. After a reasonable period of time, he resigned his position at the brokerage firm where he worked and moved east, explaining to his friends and coworkers that Houston held too many bad memories for him and his daughter."

"Cynthia found out her father killed her mother?"

"That's what we suspect. Benini wasn't clear on exactly what Cynthia knew that set Capperato off. He never told Benini, just said she was blackmailing him and needed to be shut up. Permanently. For the right price Benini didn't ask questions."

"Is Benini even really his cousin?"

"That part of his story is true. He reached out to Benini and offered to launder mob money in exchange for the new identities."

"But how does all this connect to Carmen and Betty? Why did Capperato want them dead?"

Spader and Zack exchanged another look that sent fear skittering up and down my spine. Zack reached out and took hold of my hand. "You're not going to like this part," he said.

"I'm not liking any part of this. Tell me."

Spader heaved a deep sigh. "Because your mother kept bragging about your ability to solve murders, Capperato didn't want you sticking your nose into Cynthia's death. The Hunterdon County medical examiner had ruled the death an accidental drug overdose, and that's the way he wanted it left."

"Oh my god!" My hands flew to my mouth; my eyes welled up with tears that quickly cascaded down my cheeks. "I'm responsible for Carmen's and Betty's deaths?"

Spader sucked air through his gritted teeth. "Technically,

your mother is responsible for Capperato's actions, but he wanted to make sure you were too busy snooping around murders in your own neighborhood to get involved investigating Cynthia's death. He paid Benini to knock off a couple of your neighbors and make it look like more than one killer had targeted the neighborhood.

"Benini's a film buff. He decided he'd have some fun by reenacting scenes from some of his favorite movies and TV shows. He also planted the knife in your yard and phoned in the hostage incident that led to the swatting."

I turned to face Zack. "I caused their deaths. How can I live with myself?"

"Benini killed them," he said. "On Lawrence's orders."

"But if not for me, they'd both still be alive."

Spader cleared his throat. "Not for long."

"What do you mean?" I asked.

"Benini researched the people on your street. He chose Bentworth and Cordova because both were already dying.

"Dying? They both looked perfectly healthy to me."

"Bentworth had advanced stage pancreatic cancer and had refused treatment. Mrs. Cordova had an inoperable brain tumor. She had less than a month to live. She and her family were aware of the situation."

"Great. A killer with a conscience. Is that supposed to make me feel better? Carmen suffered a horrible death."

"No, she didn't," said Spader. "All her stab wounds were postmortem. The medical examiner discovered a bullet to the back of her head. Benini stripped off her clothes, then placed her in the shower and stabbed her repeatedly. Like Bentworth, she never knew what hit her and died instantly."

I shook my head. "Small consolation, Detective. I still robbed her of what little time she had left with her family. And all because Mama bragged about me? How evil can one man be?"

"I've seen far worse," said Spader.

"Again, not helping, Detective." I turned to Zack. "Mama can never learn about this. It would kill her."

"Agreed."

~*~

I took off work the next day. Zack accompanied me to the hospital to pick up Mama and bring her home. That was the easy part. We still had to tell her about her husband—everything except the part she played in the deaths of my neighbors.

We found her sitting on a chair in front of the window in her hospital room. "I can't imagine what got into Lawrence last night," she said. "I suppose it was the shock of being mistaken for a killer, but I'm going to insist he get a complete medical check-up. He may be developing dementia or have a brain tumor. There are no other logical explanations for his behavior.

"I hope he and the police sorted everything out afterwards." She craned her neck to look behind us. "Where is he? Why isn't he with you?"

"He's in jail, Mama." I proceeded to tell her what we'd learned about her husband.

"Impossible," she said. "Lawrence is a lover, not a killer. I don't believe it. There has to be some mistake. Someone is framing him."

"Believe it, Mama. You can thank Lucille for saving your life. If she hadn't deliberately tripped him with her cane, you might have become his next victim." I have no doubt Salvatore Capperato would have gotten rid of Mama as soon as she was no longer of use to him in his getaway plan.

The thought of being indebted to Lucille caused Mama

physical pain. Her face contorted. "That pinko pig—"

"Saved your life," repeated Zack, a bit more forcefully than I had.

Mama scowled. "Well, I suppose even *she's* capable of a good deed now and then."

"The man you knew as Lawrence will spend the rest of his life behind bars. What will you do, Mama?"

"Well, I'm certainly not staying married to a killer! I suppose I'll have to divorce him." Mama had never filed for divorce. All her husbands died on her. The expression on her face told me she didn't relish the idea. "Do you think I have grounds for an annulment?"

"We'll look into it," I said, adding, "I'm sorry this marriage didn't work out for you, Mama. You seemed so happy." At least at first but I'd noticed telltale signs of unrest from the moment she and her latest husband had returned from their honeymoon.

"I am, too, dear." Mama sighed. "At least this husband didn't die on me. Perhaps the curse is broken, and I'll find my happily ever after with the next man who enters my life."

In the back of my mind I heard Ralph squawking, "*There stays a husband to make you a wife. Romeo and Juliet.* Act Two, Scene Five."

ANASTASIA'S KNIT AND CROCHETED BABY BLANKETS

KNIT BLANKETS

Abbreviations:
K=knit
P=pearl
st(s)=stitch(es)

Garter Stitch Bordered Knit Blanket

Materials: 12-oz. 4-ply knitting worsted in desired color, size 7 knitting needles

Cast on 135 sts.
Rows 1-9: K 135
Row 10: K 6, P 123, K 6
Row 11: K 123
Repeat Row 10 and 11 until blanket measures 32".
Repeat Rows 1-9.

Bind off.

Basket Weave Knit Blanket

Materials: 12-oz. 4-ply knitting worsted in desired color, size 7 knitting needles

Cast on 135 sts.
Rows 1, 3, 6, and 8: P 5 * K 5, P 5. Repeat from * across row.
Rows 2, 4, 5, and 7: K 5, * P 5, K 5. Repeat from * across row.
Repeat above eight rows until piece measures 32", ending with row 8. Bind off.

CROCHETED BLANKETS

Abbreviations:
Ch=chain
SC=single crochet
DC=double crochet
st=stitch

Super Simple Crocheted Blanket

Materials: 24-oz. 4-ply knitting worsted in desired color, #4 crochet hook

Ch 118
Row 1: Beginning with second chain from hook, work SC in each chain.
Row 2: Turn blanket. Work 1 SC in each stitch.

Repeat Row 2 until blanket measures 30".

Fasten off.

Shell Patterned Crocheted Blanket

Materials: 24-oz. 4-ply knitting worsted in desired color, #4 crochet hook

Ch 118.

Row 1: Work 1 SC in first Ch, skip 2 Ch, 6 DC in next Ch *, skip 2 Ch, 1 SC in next Ch, skip 2 Ch, 6 DC in next Ch. Repeat from *, ending row with 1 SC in last Ch. Ch 2, turn.

Row 2: * 1 DC in each DC of shell, taking up back thread only. Skip SC between shells. Repeat from *, ending 1 DC in last SC. Ch 1, turn.

Row 3: 1 sc in first dc *, 6 dc in space between third and fourth dc from sc just made. 1 sc in space between the next third and fourth dc. Repeat from * across row, ending with 1sc in last dc. Ch 2, turn.

Repeat rows 2 and 3 until piece measures 30".

Border: Work 2 rows of SC around entire blanket, working 3 SC in each corner st.

Edging: Starting on third st from corner, work 1 SC *, skip 2 sts. 6 DC in next st. Skip 2 sts. 1 SC in next st. repeat from * around entire cover, skipping only 1 st at corners. Fasten off.

ABOUT THE AUTHOR

USA Today bestselling and award-winning author Lois Winston writes mystery, romance, romantic suspense, chick lit, women's fiction, children's chapter books, and non-fiction under her own name and her Emma Carlyle pen name. *Kirkus Reviews* dubbed her critically acclaimed Anastasia Pollack Crafting Mystery series, "North Jersey's more mature answer to Stephanie Plum." In addition, Lois is an award-winning craft and needlework designer who often draws much of her source material for both her characters and plots from her experiences in the crafts industry. Visit Lois/Emma at www.loiswinston.com and Anastasia at the Killer Crafts & Crafty Killers blog, www.anastasiapollack.blogspot.com. Follow everyone on Tsu at www.tsu.co/loiswinston, on Twitter @anasleuth, and on Pinterest at www.pinterest.com/anasleuth.

To learn of new Anastasia Pollack Crafting Mystery releases as well as other new books, sign up for Lois's newsletter at her website or at:
https://www.MyAuthorBiz.com/ENewsletter.php?acct=LW246
7152513

Made in the USA
Middletown, DE
09 August 2015